OPEN SECRET

To Huw
With all my love
Mary
x x x

MARY MEDLICOTT

PONT BOOKS

First Impression – 2004

ISBN 1 84323 289 8

This book is published with the financial support of the
Welsh Books Council.

Printed in Wales at
Gomer Press, Llandysul, Ceredigion, Wales.

For Paul

1

I stopped in my tracks when the girl appeared – as if freezing on the spot could stop her from seeing me. It was habit, I suppose. Don't be noticed, don't stand out: it had become like second nature.

The girl was trying to close the door of the cottage, but it was obviously hard to get it shut. With both hands grasping the doorknob, she tried slamming it again and again. I could see she was a girl, no problem, although her hair was short and she was wearing jeans. I thought she had to be about my age and I definitely didn't want her to see me.

I thought of turning and running for cover. So I glanced towards the forest, checking if I could get back there without being spotted. But I'd come further away from the trees than I thought and the track where I was standing was stony: it was bound to sound crunchy if I started to run.

Suddenly it was too late to try. I heard the slam of the cottage door as the girl finally succeeded and when I looked back, she was turning onto the gravel path that led down the hillside away from the little whitewashed house. The track I was on met the path from the house just at the point where it widened and, from the way they curved into each other, I knew she was going to see me.

She was running by now as if she was in a hurry and had something urgent to do. Suddenly she was looking straight at me.

'Aaah!' She came to a screeching stop, covering her mouth with her hands as she spoke. '*Sori. Ces i sioc. Pwy wyt ti? Beth wyt ti'n 'neud yn sefyll fanna?*'

She stared at me like I was someone that had just dropped down from the stars. When I didn't answer, she tried again, this time speaking in English. She wanted to know what I was doing, standing there staring. I stayed rooted to the spot.

'Don't you talk Welsh then?' she added after a moment, speaking in a lilty Welsh accent. 'Or maybe you don't talk at all?' She smiled, disarmingly.

She didn't get any answer from me, and she didn't get a chance to say any more either because suddenly, quick as a flash, I was off. I couldn't face it a second longer. I couldn't deal with her or her questions. I had no idea who she was or anything about her, though I probably thought she lived somewhere nearby, perhaps not in the tumbledown cottage on top of the hill but maybe somewhere out of sight down the hillside. I wasn't going to wait to find out.

I ran as fast as I could, off the track towards the trees, then slipping and sliding down the steep slope through the forest. The earth was wet and thick with leaves and the first bit was like going down a slide in a playground. Afterwards I bumped along, half the time on my bottom, only managing to steady up when I came to the thicker part of the forest where the ground was a bit less steep. My heart was pounding, thudding and pounding, and my stomach was churned up, just as it had felt on that other occasion when I'd been seen by the creepy man in the lane. That was when I'd

8

understood how important it was for me not to be seen, not just for everyone else's sake but for mine as well.

Eventually I came down through the bottom part of the forest towards my den, my mind still full of the girl up the top. As I picked my way through the trees close to the den, I kept seeing her picture in the front of my mind, her hands flying up to her mouth, wide-eyed with the surprise of seeing me.

Maybe one shock produces another, like when dominoes start to tumble, each one setting the next one off. Anyway, when I was close to my den, I slipped and fell, splat, into the mud. My mind was fixed on the girl on the hill. I could still see her face, I could see her surprised expression and I realized as I zoomed in on my snapshot that I could even see freckles on her nose.

That's when I found myself sliding. It was like I was on a banana-skin carpet. It happened so fast I hardly knew anything about it until I landed on my backside in the middle of the mud. As I landed, I felt two or three splodges shoot up and arrive on my face, and that's when I knew it was that thick mucky sort of mud that sticks to you all over. Then, of course, I managed to make things worse by putting my hands up to wipe the mess off my face.

Handfuls of damp grass don't do much for muddy trousers – or hands, or trainers. After a while, I gave up trying to get myself clean and, instead of going across to my den, carried on to Greenland.

2

'God, Charlie! What a mess!' It was Jeremy. He'd been bending over a pile of logs on the forest side of the woodstore and he was holding some of them against his chest, obviously to carry them into the shed. As he raised himself to his full height, he looked even more awkward and gangly than usual. 'Been taking a mud-bath, have we?' he called, staring across at me with his lop-sided smile. 'Anyway, it's good to see you. And when you've got a minute – when you've changed will do, presuming you are going to change, of course? – come and help me carry these logs in, will you?'

I was lucky. Jeremy was not in one of his talkative moods and there was no one else in sight. I carried on past the woodstore and went round the back of the farmhouse and straight towards the yurt where I sleep and where I've always had my own special place.

A yurt is a kind of tent and this one's made like ones they've got in Mongolia. I like it. Outside, you always feel like there might be magic inside and inside, it's shadowy and peaceful, especially when it's getting dark in the evenings.

After taking off my muddy trainers on my way into the yurt, I peered through the embroidered flap which acts like an inner door and quickly looked around inside, hoping that none of the others would be there. Inside, everything was quiet, no flickering movements among the strange shadows that fall on the groundsheet from the clothes we keep hanging on the ropes up above.

No one was inside, I made sure of that. 'Irina?' I called. No answer came. 'Dad?' Again nothing, so I went right into the yurt and crossed to my own private section which is a kind of little room, divided from the rest by hangings. Quickly I opened my clothes chest, the wooden one Dad made me when I first came to Greenland, and grabbed my clogs off the tray that's like a shelf at the top of the chest. My clogs are great. I wear them instead of slippers when I go for a shower or when I go out to the toilet.

I fetched one of the baskets that we generally keep next to the wood-stove so they're warm and dry and ready for using, grabbed clean clothes, my towel and wash-bag and quietly slipped out of the yurt, checking as I went that there was still no one else around. I threw my clogs down on the grass, shoved my feet inside them and crossed the field to the shower-tent as fast as I could.

The shower-tent is fantastic. If you don't know anything about the amazing amount of heat you can get from the sun, and the way you can use it to heat up water, you probably wouldn't believe how warm the water in that shower can be. It's brilliant! Of course, it should be. It's been rigged up by experts.

It was while I was in the shower, washing the mud off me in that lovely warm water, that I first realised for sure that I'd be going back up to the cottage. I'd go there, I decided, at the first chance I could get. When I got up through the forest, I'd wait around till I was sure no one was around, then this time I'd see if I could manage to get a peek inside the building.

3

I suppose that's where this story of mine really begins. It wasn't that I necessarily wanted to see the girl again. I just wanted to get acquainted with the boundaries of my new world.

You see, Greenland is about as different from London as I think the moon must be from the earth. Put it another way. In Greenland, I've had to learn everything from scratch, like I was some kind of infant creature who has just started getting used to life on one planet when he's dumped in another.

I've been here now for almost a year but the day I first saw Megan, it'd only been a couple of months. I still vividly remember arriving and what life was like at the start. It's in my head like it happened yesterday.

We travelled here on a Wednesday. The day before, in the evening, Dad and I had gone round to Mum's. That was fine, better than I'd expected, because Mum and I had already said our proper goodbyes after we'd made the final decision about where I was going to live. Even the deciding had not been too hard because by the time it happened, Mum and Dad had both had their own separate places for quite a while. I'd been living part of the week with Mum, the rest with Dad, and I'd got used to the routine.

What made the change was when Dad started spending lots more time out of London. You can't blame him. He'd been interested in woods and forests for ages. Then after meeting Jeremy, the guy that started Greenland, Dad really got into the country in a very big way. He started telling me a lot about this valley in Wales where Jeremy lived, and I remember getting very confused about how come it was called Greenland. I remember asking him, 'Dad, I thought Greenland was near the North Pole?' But Dad explained that this place was in south west Wales and it was called Glastir in Welsh, Greenland in English.

It didn't take long before the big questions came up. Who goes where? What's going to happen to Charlie? Will it be better for him to go to Wales to live in Greenland or to stay in London?

'All I want,' I remember Mum saying, 'is whatever's best for Charlie.' I remember her saying it over and over. 'I only want what's best for him.'

That's when the decision was finally made that I'd go to Greenland to live. I'd already been to visit with Dad, to see if I would like it and to meet Jeremy and the others, and Dad was really, really happy when it came to the point and I said I would go. He said it would be a healthy, happy life.

The day before we left London for good, Dad had to rush about doing last-minute jobs and finish packing up things in his flat. He'd decided he wouldn't get rid of the flat just yet, in case things didn't work out in Greenland. Instead he'd decided to rent it out and he'd found an agent to handle the business. But he still had to leave the place tidy and lock up the stuff he wouldn't be needing in the cupboard at the end of the hall.

By the time Dad was finished, it was a close run thing for us not to be late to Mum's. The last thing we did before going over to her place was to put out the sleeping bags so we could get into them quickly when we came back and have a good night's sleep before setting out early in the morning.

Mum had done a really great meal. You could smell it as you came through the front door – spaghetti bolognese, my favourite. For afters, there was ice-cream, Cookies and Cream, my best sort. After we'd finished eating and Dad and Mum were having coffee, we talked about when she'd come to Greenland to see me. She said she probably wouldn't come for Christmas. 'You know me, I feel the cold,' she said, all the time pretending to shiver, making a thing of it like grown-ups do. 'Anyway,' she went on, 'perhaps you should come up to London for Christmas. As for me coming down, perhaps I should come before then.' She mentioned the Autumn, maybe October, as a good time for her to visit and see how I was getting on.

When we were doing the washing up, just Mum and me in the kitchen together, Mum said she had something important to give me. She reached down a piece of paper from one of the shelves and as she handed it to me, I saw she'd written some numbers on it. 'My new mobile phone number,' she said, giving me a special hug. 'I know they don't have phones in Greenland, but you never know, there might be some time when you need it.' I put the paper in my pocket and, after that, I always kept it on me.

After we'd finished washing up, I sat down on the sofa in the living room for a while before Mum and I had to say goodbye. Thomas, that's our old cat, was sitting at one end, curled round on the cushion so you

14

could hardly see he had legs or a head. He just looked like a ball of orange fur. I started tickling him on the ear where he likes it and then he started to stretch, as if he was saying, 'What's happening now?'

As I kept on, Thomas slowly opened one eye and looked up. When he knew it was me, he started purring straight away. Then he curled himself round again and went back to sleep. I took this as a compliment. It's not that he didn't want to give me any attention. It's like I was still part of the furniture.

When it was time to go, it was fine actually saying goodbye. Mum gave me a huge big hug, then held me away from her briefly and looked at me sideways like only she can – like she really knows me and is thinking she might have something extra to say but then decides it doesn't need saying. Instead she hugged me all over once more and sort of wiped a tear from her eye. Then suddenly she was laughing and making little jokes and telling me to remember to wash my ears. Never mind my feet, just my ears.

'Why's that, Mum?' I asked. 'Why not my feet?'

'No,' she said, 'it's only that you're specially going to need your ears to hear that I'm thinking about you, silly.'

Then we were on our way. As Dad and I were getting ready to go out the front door, Mum reached her hand into the big hall cupboard. 'Something else for you,' she said, reaching out a smart new backpack filled to bursting with the stuff inside it. She said it was things she'd got together that she thought I might like – random stuff, she said, from socks to cakes. Oh, and a nice thick warm jumper to add to my wardrobe, and three packets of my favourite biscuits.

She wouldn't let me actually open the pack while I was there on the doorstep. I didn't do that till the morning, back at Dad's. When I woke early and couldn't get back to sleep, sorting through it was something to pass the time till Dad woke up. Besides, I wanted to see everything that was in it and I couldn't wait to get to the bottom: it was like opening your Christmas stocking.

4

The longest part of the journey was on the motorway, the M4. I didn't bother about it really, just listened to my tapes and talked to Dad a bit in between. The van was loaded to the roof and it chugged every time we went up a slight hill. But when we came to the Severn Bridge, it just swooshed across as if the bridge was the ocean and the van was a tall-masted ship in one of those round-the-world races that you see on TV.

The bridge looked pretty. I hadn't seen it before. The last time I'd been to Wales, the time when we went to see if I really wanted to go and live there, I was fast asleep when we got to the bridge. The time before that, when Dad himself was still trying to make up his mind about living in Greenland full-time, we'd gone another way – over the old bridge. This time I specially looked out to get a sight of the old bridge in the distance as we sailed over the new one.

This time, too, when we were half-way across, I realised I was feeling excited about going to live in a different country. I wanted to say something to celebrate and I really wished I knew something in Welsh. That's when I thought about Dacky. Dacky was my granddad and that's what I used to call him, Dacky, though I realise now that the proper word is Dad-cu.

Dacky used to live in South Wales with Nain (that was my Welsh Granny, and I remember for ages seeing her name in my head as Nine.) When they were still alive, they sometimes used to come up to London to visit, and when they did it was always a great event. Sometimes, even better, we used to go down to Wales to stay with them, me and Dad and Mum. One time when I was a little boy, we were visiting their house, which was near an old coal-mine, and Dacky and me were playing out in the garden when one of the neighbours came walking along. He was an old bloke too and he stopped to talk to my granddad. The two of them leaned on the gate for ages, chatting, and then I remember them calling me over and Dacky teaching me these words, '*Bore da*'. He said I should say them whenever I wanted to say Hello to someone in Wales in the morning.

So that's what I said as we went over the last part of the Severn bridge in the van. I said it out loud. '*Bore da*, Wales. Good morning.'

My father laughed. 'You still remember what Dad-cu taught you, then? It's going to come in handy from now on, isn't it?'

That didn't turn out to be true, by the way, not for

17

ages, because until I met Megan, I never knew anyone I could try the words out on.

From the bridge, it was still going to be a long journey to Greenland. But at least we'd eventually be heading off the M4. I was keeping my eyes on the signposts. Mostly I couldn't make them out because I had no idea how to read the Welsh. I felt sad about not being able to say the place names, even in my head.

The rainbow, though, was great. The sky had darkened after we came off the bridge. Then it got even greyer and suddenly it was raining cats and dogs and you know whenever anyone says that, I always think about my cat Thomas. I imagine him falling out of the sky in a bundle and I try and think what he would look like. Would his legs stretch out in every direction? And what about his tail? And what if there were loads of Thomases, hundreds and thousands of them falling together? And dogs as well? Would they start fighting as they plummeted down? Or would they be too stunned?

When the downpour finally stopped, Dad turned off the windscreen wipers. It was a relief to stop their squeaking. Then the sun burst out from behind the clouds, like all the lights in a football stadium flashing on together. Dad immediately said, 'There'll be a good rainbow somewhere, I bet.'

And there it was, straight ahead like a welcoming arch. For a while it kept moving, like it was leading us into the middle of Wales. Then it seemed to stop and I was sure we must be going underneath it, except when I turned and squinted through the back window to try and see it again, it had completely disappeared.

5

We stopped for some lunch at a place called Crosshands.

'What d'you want, luv?' the waitress asked. I chose a cheese sandwich and a jam tart and Lilt.

'Goin' on your holidays then, are you?' She was a middle-aged, friendly type with mousey-brown hair where it grew out of her head but bright yellow everywhere else.

'Not exactly,' I replied.

'Oh?' said the waitress, waiting for me to say a bit more. 'Where you goin', then, if you don't mind me asking?'

Dad piped up. 'To see friends for a while, stay with them, help out a bit. In the country, Carmarthen way.'

She seemed happy with that. But Dad must have noticed I was feeling uneasy because afterwards, when the waitress went off to fetch what we wanted, he started talking again about the secrecy thing and why we had to be careful how much we said about Greenland. I knew a lot about the reasons. They'd been part of the discussions when we visited and afterwards talking with Mum about whether I'd actually live there. I don't know why Dad had to raise it again in the café. I thought I'd done pretty well with the waitress but I suppose he couldn't help thinking about it.

'Nothing wrong with what we're doing, Charlie,' Dad explained. 'No need to feel awkward about it. Think positive. We're building for the future, building for ourselves. Finding out how to live. And if we have to keep quiet about it, that will only given us a better chance to get on with the job without anyone interfering. Planners! Inspectors! Regulators! You know what bureaucracy's like. But there's no need to feel awkward about our side of things, not at all.'

Bureaucracy is one of Dad's favourite words. Both times we'd been there together, I'd heard him going on about it. Every meal-time with the other people, Jeremy and Bridget and John and Viv, and Greg and Nuala when they were there, he'd talk about their plans for Greenland and the kind of life they were trying to make. It was obvious they all felt the same, that if they were going to do what they dreamed of, we would all have to try and avoid attracting attention from anyone in the outside world. We certainly wouldn't want any officials coming nosing about and checking up on us. The bureaucrats, Dad called them, spitting out the word. To him, to all of them, bureaucrats were the most important reason why Greenland had to be kept secret.

When the waitress came back and Dad was paying the bill, she started talking to me again. 'Been down this way before then, have we?'

'Only a couple of times,' I replied. 'But it's OK, I like it. So I'm glad we're coming back.'

That made her smile and I suddenly liked her better until, unfortunately, she put out her hand and ruffled my hair. I know mine's curly, but honestly, you'd think people would know better.

After Crosshands, the sun was shining and the countryside got a lot more interesting. It was different here from the part of the country where Dacky and Nine used to live. That was where there had been coal mines and houses in rows up the valley. But here was mostly fields with cows and sheep and every now and again, someone out walking, or kids on bikes, or someone riding a horse. When we came to the horse, we had to slow down so it wouldn't be frightened.

The van wasn't too happy whenever we went up a hill, but at least it didn't conk out. Then Dad said I should start looking out for the turning to Greenland. I was really pleased when I recognised the village where we had to turn off onto a minor road: there's not much there except for some houses, each on its own with a little garden in front, and a big square chapel set back from the road. Apart from that, there's only a crossroads with a phone box, a petrol station and a village shop. That's how I managed to recognise it.

Past the village we turned off onto the small country road and went bundling down into a pretty little valley. Almost immediately we were chugging up the other side and I saw that we had reached Pen-y-Cwm, the little place that is nearest to Greenland. As soon as I saw the signpost, I recognised the name because Dad had talked to me about it.

Pen-y-Cwm is even smaller than the village before it, but it still has its own chapel. As we drove past, I tried reading the plaque above the door. I'd already decided that, coming to live here, I'd have to try learning all I could about the area. We were going a bit too fast for me to see more than one word in big letters, Salem. It wasn't until a long time later that I finally managed to work the rest out – Eglwys y Bedyddwyr, Baptist Chapel.

A kilometre or so out of Pen-y-Cwm, I was suddenly shouting, 'Dad, Dad, there's our turning.' But of course Dad was already manouvering the van into the side-road before I'd even managed to get the words out. I was forgetting that he'd already been here many more times than I had: this was where he'd come to live.

6

By now, the sun had come out strongly and the hedges cast dark shadows on the roads. Even so, it was quite a shock when we bumped off the road onto the stony track down to the settlement. Where the trees begin, a little way down the track, it looked quite dark and where they grow together over the road, making a kind of arch, it looked like we had to drive through a tunnel. It reminded me of the rainbow after we'd crossed the bridge into Wales.

The first thing I saw when our van came out the other side of the trees and drove through the gate into Greenland was Mollie. As we drew to a halt, she was racing towards us, woof-woofing and wagging her tail.

Viv and John were coming out of the farmhouse, arms twined round each other, their free arms waving, and their twins running after them, shouting and laughing. I felt really happy. Everyone was in a good mood and I felt I'd come home.

Viv and John were the first to reach us as we climbed out of the van. Viv hardly looks like a mother, she seems so young. I noticed that they were both wearing exactly the same clothes as when I'd said goodbye the last time: baggy denim dungarees with big patch pockets and check shirts underneath. They've both got the same blond hair as well.

'Hiya,' called Viv with a little grin, 'how's things?'

John didn't say much, he doesn't go in for talking, but it was great to see him again. As he and Viv started hugging me and Dad, shaking our hands and squeezing our arms, their little boy, Ben, started grabbing my jeans and pulling himself up onto my legs and my chest. It was fun. Ben had got into doing that the last time I was there and I liked him trusting me not to let him fall.

Then Hannah, Ben's twin, started trying to do the same. She was still trying to pull him out of the way and get a hold on me when suddenly he pushed her, I think by accident. Anyway, she fell over and hit the ground with a bump and then, of course, she started to cry. Viv picked her up and John scooped Ben up onto his shoulders. Hannah's crying had brought out the others.

'Hi there, folks!' came Greg's familiar New Zealand voice and when I looked round, there he was, his arm round Nuala's shoulder, grinning all over his face. Nuala's Irish and she's got pale, pale skin. Her stomach was enormous, like a huge big balloon, so I didn't need to ask to know that her baby hadn't arrived yet. Funny, I'd been wondering about it on the way down in the car and I felt pleased when I realised that now I'd be in Greenland when the baby was born.

'Hi, Charlie,' Greg said, grinning and sticking his hand out to take hold of mine. But I know better than to put my hand in his. His grip is like iron, and he's always trying to trick me.

'Na,' I said, shaking my head and laughing, 'I'll shake hands with you tomorrow.'

'OK, Charlie, I'll hold you to that,' Greg drawled. 'How're you doing, anyway? Been down any good waves lately?'

That's the thing about Greg, he's fantastically tough and incredibly sporty. He does climbing and kayaking and coasteering, you name it. And he'd already said that, if I wanted, he'd take me on some of the courses he runs. 'Kayaking's my best thing,' I told him the last time I saw him. 'Oh, yea?' he said. 'And how's it going?' When I told him I was getting on well with my Eskimo rolls, he actually looked impressed.

I was taking another glance at Nuala's big stomach and wondering if her baby was going to look like her when I saw my pet hate, Amy, coming over the field towards us. In front of her was Jeremy, her father, and while he strode along quickly on his long gangly legs, she lagged behind like she didn't want to be going anywhere. I didn't think that was surprising. Amy and I just do not get on. She's too sulky for me and I suppose I'm too much of a dreamer for her. She's always moaning at me. Why don't I do this? Why don't I do that? Why don't I let on what I'm thinking?

Why Amy even bothered to come out to say hello beats me. I suppose Jeremy insisted. He likes doing things properly. He's a bit of an egg-head, one with a wispy beard, and although he means well, he sometimes gets on my nerves. I really went off him when I started living in Greenland. He's the ideas-man and everyone else sort of listens to him – everyone except for Amy, she just listens to him when she wants to. When she finally got close to the place where we were all chatting, she didn't even say hello. Instead, she turned to Nuala like she was deliberately ignoring me, then drew Nuala down towards her, cupped her mouth under Nuala's long black hair and whispered something secret in her ear. Nuala just smiled sweetly at her with her smiley blue eyes, then turned away and carried on talking to Dad and me.

Jeremy wanted to know if we'd had a good journey. 'Van holding out?' he said to Dad. 'Brought all your stuff?' he said to me. Then he turned back to Dad and, in that intense way that he has, immediately started asking Dad if he'd been able to bring him some books they'd obviously been discussing the last time they spoke. When Dad said yes, Jeremy looked delighted, as if he'd quite like to go off and start reading them at once. Nothing would have suited him more, I expect. Instead he astonished me by declaring in a friendly way that we should all go in and have some tea. 'Celebration time,' he added.

'And Matthew?' I was asking on our way to the farmhouse. 'Isn't Matthew here today?' But before anyone could answer, someone I'd never seen before was rushing out towards us. She hadn't been there the other two times I visited Greenland and she was the most amazing-looking person I'd ever set eyes on, all skirts and bright colours and scarves and red hair, and everything swirling around in a kind of whirlwind of laughing. She had a big husky voice, but funny and nice, and an amazing way of talking, not English or Welsh or anything I could recognise. Maybe she was Russian, I said to myself, and I turned out to be right.

'Zis must be Charlie – CHARRRLIE – how are you CHARRLIE?' She came forward in a dash and without waiting for anyone to introduce us, she swallowed me up in a huge big hug. With anyone else I'd have hated it, but somehow it was OK with her.

'Charlie, this is Irina,' Viv butted in quickly, untangling herself from Hannah who'd suddenly stopped crying. 'She's only been here with us for a week so far, but she's going to stay for a while, aren't you, Irina? At least till Nuala's had her baby . . . or maybe longer, hey, Irina?' Viv laughed as she turned back towards the amazing woman. 'We'd like to have you forever, Irina.'

But Irina wasn't listening. She'd already moved on to hugging Dad. 'So ZIS is Charlie's FA-A-THER,' – she drew all her words out – 'so G-L-AA-D to zee you, g-l-aa-d to zee you.'

Dad looked a teensy bit embarrassed as Irina squeezed his shoulder. 'You must be the person Jeremy mentioned before I left to go and fetch Charlie,' he muttered. 'You obviously got here safely, and I'm sure Nuala must be feeling glad to have you here, aren't you Nuala? Nice to meet you, anyway, and welcome, welcome . . .'

It turned out over tea that Irina is a midwife, so

obviously she knows all about babies. I was soon to discover how many other things she knows besides. She's an amazing cook and she makes everything she wears, and she's also a bit of an artist and the best person in the world for knowing things without showing off. Irina knows about everything, countries and languages and history and stories. She's a sort of walking treasure-house and it's never just book-stuff, not with Irina. She's actually been to nearly all the places she talks about, she's seen the paintings, she's walked round the buildings, and she's talked to all the people.

I loved Irina right from the start. It seemed the most amazing beginning to my new life, having Irina for a friend. And that's what she was from the first, a friend. She still is, even though now she's on her travels again and we can only keep in touch through letters. Actually, at the moment, until she settles in one place for a bit, I can't write to her, she can only write to me. But I don't mind too much because I know I'll see her again. Also I just love it when Dad or one of the others comes back from our PO Box in Carmarthen with a letter addressed to me from her. It's never in one of those blue air-mail envelopes with the red zig-zag lines round the edges. Her envelopes are always big and coloured and they've always got an interesting stamp in the corner. The last one she sent was from Japan and it had a drawing of a *tengu* on the back. That's the other thing I appreciate about Irina's envelopes: they always have a weird drawing on the back that she's made specially for me. Maybe it'll be a lizard or a cat or a monkey. Or maybe even a *tengu*. And of course I'd never have known what a *tengu* is if it wasn't for Irina. A *tengu*, she told me in the letter, is a peculiar Japanese demon that can fly through the air and has an extremely long nose.

7

Living in Greenland soon settled into its own very special no-routine routine. There was no school, for a start, at least not in the way I'd been used to. For the first few days I kept thinking of Dan and Wayne turning up with the others at my old school gate, kicking a football around the playground, then going into class. I wondered which classes they'd be in this term, if they'd be in different classes or all together like we were before.

Somehow it was very different, playing football in Greenland with Matthew. Matthew's crazy about the game, like me, and he's really, really good. But he's a whole year younger than I am and, though we get on fine, it wasn't quite the same as mucking about with my London mates. Besides, whenever we set up a game, kicking goals or practising ball-skills, there'd always be Hannah and Ben wanting to join in too. And Mollie the dog would often get in the way. Mollie's a little Jack Russell. She's fun, except when you want a serious game.

In Greenland there were no classes. We just learned

about whatever we were interested in and the grown-ups taught us the things they liked best. From day one, I did a lot of building, mainly on the new wooden house which Jeremy had designed for Greg and Nuala, but also on odd jobs at the farmhouse and on Jeremy and Bridget's roundhouse. I haven't mentioned Bridget before. She's Jeremy's partner and she's a professional potter and she's often away from Greenland, delivering her products around the country to the shops and centres where she sells them. She was actually away from Greenland the day I arrived. When she got back, it was the first time I saw her in her new red glasses. They suit her, the glasses, they're whacky like her.

The roundhouse where Bridget lives with Jeremy is made all of wood and fantastic inside with different nooks for sleeping and living and hundreds of little shelves and hooks for hanging things from. There's an area for cooking, another for washing, and Amy and Matthew each have their own separate spaces the other side of the raised platform area where Bridget and Jeremy sleep. Matthew has decorated every inch of his space with football posters and stickers. Bridget just laughs and says he'll have to build his own roundhouse soon if he wants to put up any more.

Greg and Nuala's new house was being built against the hillside at the far end of the meadow the other side of the farmhouse. There was already a big rush to try and get it finished in time for Nuala's baby when Dad and I got to Greenland to live; there was still a lot to do on it. I liked seeing it develop as the days went by and I couldn't wait for the roof to go on. I knew about the

plan to grass it over so as to help to keep the heat in –
and by now, by the way, it looks really beautiful. The
grass has grown tall and, when there's a breeze, it
waves about like a person's hair. Sometimes it's full of
flowers. In fact, I remember Bridget scattering flower
seeds on the turves when we'd finally finished laying
them all over the roof. 'You wait and see,' she said to
Nuala. 'The roof will be blooming by the time that
baby of yours starts crawling.'

Greg and Nuala were desperate to move out of their
old bus, so a lot of our energies were spent on their
house. But there were still jobs to be done on the old
farmhouse too. Viv and John were in charge over there.
John is an expert carpenter and he and Viv had already
finished installing the solar panels to collect the sun off
the roof before I came to Greenland. Now they still had
one last section of roofing to do. I got really used to
seeing one or other of them up on the ladder. 'Hiya!
How's things?' Viv would smile down as I passed. John
would just nod in a friendly kind of way, then put up
his hand to push his hair away from his eyes.

Inside the farmhouse, there were other tasks like
finishing the shelving and the cupboards. I had to get
good at handling wood, cutting, measuring and all that
sort of stuff. It made me learn a lot about practical
maths, though I could never do as well as Matthew on
measuring things. He may be just a kid but he really
loves his maths. It's what he likes best, apart from his
football.

Another activity I began doing in Greenland was
making pots with Bridget. She got me making dishes

and bowls to start off with and soon I was trying my hand at plates and mugs as well. Bridget's incredibly involved with her work and at the same time she's down-to-earth despite being a bit zany every now and again. Sometimes I wonder how she puts up with Jeremy when he's being extra stuffy and going on about his great ideas.

Mostly Bridget makes pots for using, not just for looking pretty. She has a potter's wheel that you work by foot and when it comes to glazing the pots, she manages to get beautiful colours. Some of the craft shops and markets where she takes her stuff are quite a long way from Greenland and she's got a regular round that she keeps to. Often she takes Amy or Matthew with her, though never the two of them at once. I suppose that's understandable since, although they don't quarrel, they don't have much to do with each other either, despite living in the same place. You see, Bridget isn't Amy's mother and Jeremy's not Matthew's dad and it's only a couple of years since Amy and Matthew started having to practise being brother and sister.

Then there was Irina. Just talking to Irina was fantastic. But we also did special lessons together. She never called any subject by its name, we just studied it like you would want to, because it was interesting. Most days Amy and Matthew joined in, especially when we were doing geography or art. Ben and Hannah usually came too when we were painting or drawing. But I always liked it best when it was just Irina and me doing extra French. That's because I already knew a lot of French from the time Mum and me spent two whole summers in a cottage in a little French village.

In Greenland every day has a sort of pattern where everybody gets up earlier than we ever used to in London. Except in the summer, we all go to bed earlier too, with the grown-ups often going to bed quite soon after the kids. Everyone has jobs, the children as well as the grown-ups. Apart from Ben and Hannah, who are too young, we all help with cooking joint meals in the farmhouse where we always have supper together. We also all help with the washing-up and the weeding and cleaning the shower-tent; things like that.

All of us in Greenland also have our own spaces which we look after ourselves. Like I said before, my private space is in the big yurt in the meadow. At first it was strange trying to get to sleep in there, even though Dad has his bed there too. But I soon started to love it, especially the cloths that hang down from the roof-space, making different compartments. The cloths we've got are lovely to look at because they have these beautiful patterns and you can see all kinds of shapes in the designs. I remember the first time I began noticing the animals' faces and weird sorts of plants, even magical islands. I was surprised I hadn't spotted them before when I was visiting. Nor did I see them the first couple of nights after I'd come to live there. I suppose it took a few nights to settle into the magic.

Besides the yurt where Dad and I sleep and where there's a separate space for visitors like Irina, Greenland had two other yurts by the time I came there to live. One is where John and Viv live with Ben and Hannah and Mollie. It's a bit smaller than ours and closer to the farmhouse, and it's full of wooden toys for Ben and Hannah to play with. Ben and Hannah are only four and John is potty about them. He loves making things for them to play with. He's made a spinning-top, a train and a spinning man and also a kind of wendy-house with a whole set of puppet figures. Irina calls Ben and Hannah the blessed twins because they're always so happy and smiling – except when one of them is crying.

The third yurt is a small one. It's down beside the river that flows past our meadow and people can go inside it either to meditate or just be quiet. Even us kids go there sometimes, which some people may think is odd. Actually it can be really good. When you get cross or upset and you go and sit inside for a while, you'll probably start feeling all right again, except that it didn't work at all for me when things started going wrong in Greenland.

8

The bad stuff started when I began my exploring after a couple of weeks had gone by. Until then, I was too busy getting into the way of things. Once a week, for instance, there was shopping to do. We usually go to Carmarthen, which is a very small place compared to London but enormous compared with any of the villages in the area. We don't usually go on Saturdays like most families would. Without school days to think about, we can go when we like, and we mostly go on market-day, which is Wednesday.

At first I used to look forward to our weekly visit to Carmarthen market. There were things there I'd never seen in London, especially the piles of cockles that had been collected on nearby beaches. Also for a while there was a stall selling laverbread, which is a kind of seaweed that you cook and eat and it doesn't look like bread at all. I'd never even heard of laverbread before, so we had to buy some for me to try. Yuk! After tasting it the first time, I never wanted to see it again. It looks disgusting and it tastes revolting.

Also there were cake stalls with cakes I'd never even heard of either such as Bara Brith and Teisen Lap. I used to stand there looking at the labels and trying to work out how to say the words. Dad wasn't much help, he'd get impatient, and anyway I used to get embarrassed at not being able to pronounce the names. But at first I wondered which ones would taste best and once or twice we bought one. They were always sweet and very filling and one day, after a couple of weeks, I asked Viv, who was with me, if we could buy a Welsh cook-book so we could try making them ourselves. Viv's the number one cake-maker in Greenland and she was happy to get some new recipes. 'OK,' she said with a little grin. Afterwards, we started trying the recipes out together and now I can do some of them really well, especially this one called Bara One-Two. In fact, I've started fancying myself as a bit of a baker.

I didn't go to Carmarthen much after the first few times, even though it had been really exciting. Every week, there was a card or a letter from Mum in the post office where we go to pick up our mail. You get your mail out of these locker-type boxes which you open with a key, and I love sorting through our stuff and seeing Mum's writing. The things she says, it's as if I can hear her speaking to me. 'And a big purr from Thomas,' she always puts at the end and I get this picture in my head of Thomas curled up on the sofa. I stopped liking Carmarthen when the novelty wore off. Funny that, because although it's minuscule compared with London, I soon discovered it was too big for me. People used to look at me oddly, like they were wondering why I was in town on a weekday and why I wasn't at school. So I generally preferred staying at home in Greenland except when the shopping was going to be in Newcastle Emlyn. That's another town, smaller than Carmarthen and a different kind of place. I like it better. It's a funny mixture of old-fashioned Welsh and what my mum calls woo-woo stuff such as scented candles and droopy clothes made from Indian cotton with shiny mirror-bits sewn on. It's also got a ruined castle and one time, I sent Mum a postcard of it. I didn't bother signing my name. I just wrote: 'Old castle in Newcastle – get it?'

One strange thing when we went to town was that I didn't have any interest in meeting people my own age, not in Carmarthen or Newcastle Emlyn or the villages closer to home. I felt shy, like they'd think me peculiar, living in Greenland and being English. Even having had two Welsh grandparents like Dacky and Nain didn't qualify me in my mind to call myself a local. So what with one thing and another, I didn't try meeting anyone new. Anyway, there weren't really many chances.

I did my exploring at home. You can do that when you've got a whole valley with fields and a river and your very own hills. One of the projects I soon got into was making a sort of map of Greenland with drawings of the different sections. The idea first came up one day when I was listening to Jeremy going on about ways of managing our Greenland resources. I found myself getting a bit irritated with him and thinking – but not saying – that it might be useful to know exactly what was there to start with. So that night when Dad and I were going to bed, I started discussing my ideas about mapping the whole area. Dad said it sounded like a really useful project and the next day, he raised it with Jeremy when we were all having supper. 'What do you think, Jeremy? Good idea?' he enquired and when Jeremy agreed, I felt quite pleased. I didn't even mind when Jeremy suggested I should start with the area nearest the farmhouse, namely the yard and outbuildings, and the big meadow where the yurts and the roundhouse are.

'Give yourself time, Charlie,' Jeremy laughed when I raised the question of the woodlands the other side of the river. 'There's a lot to learn about mapping. Start with the places you can easily reach.'

Of course, I wasn't going to be content with that. I knew I wanted to get over the river and start exploring the hillside the other side. Another problem that came up right away was Matthew. As soon as my project was mentioned, his ears pricked up and he started sounding keen to get involved. 'Hey, Charlie,' he said, putting down his pudding spoon. 'Can I help you on that? There'd be a lot of measuring and I could do the sums.'

I don't know why, but the last thing I wanted was anyone else hanging around on my project. It's not that I didn't like Matthew. I did. But the mapping was my own idea and I wanted to do it all on my own. So I put Matthew off by looking vague and distant and saying that maybe he could get involved later.

I started the very next day. I had plenty of other things on the go at the time. Mum was due to be visiting soon. Greg was talking about taking me and Matthew on an abseiling course in north Wales, and we both thought that sounded like really good fun. Besides, Bridget was planning an experiment of firing some pots under a bonfire in the field to see how they would turn out. All of us kids were going to make special pots to go in the pit and I had a good idea for mine. But no matter how busy I was going to be, I wanted to start my exploring. And that was how I came to know Megan. But not until some other things had happened that caused me a lot of grief.

9

One afternoon I was walking up the lane the other side of the Greenland gate. That's where the trees bend over the track and make it feel like a tunnel. I'd got the idea that the first target for my mapping was to get some kind of view from above of our entire valley, something that would connect it all up in my head, the old farmhouse, the fields, the woodlands, the river, everything.

So I decided to go up the lane out of Greenland and explore the road at the top. I wanted to see if I could find a bird's eye view of our valley from some point along the road. I'd already walked up there once before on my own, not long after arriving in Greenland. That time, I'd turned right at the junction and walked quite a long way along the road before realising I wasn't going to get any kind of view on that side. The trees were all too thick. Now I decided I'd try again and this time, when I got to the top of the track, I'd turn left.

It was quite hot and steamy that day, I remember, but I can't remember exactly which day of the week it was. It was after lunch, I do know that. I set off carrying my small knapsack, my daysack, with my drawing stuff and Dad's binoculars inside. I hadn't told anyone exactly what I was planning. Dad was spending the afternoon in the library in Carmarthen and everyone else was busy. Matthew was helping Greg and Jeremy on Greg and Nuala's new house, Amy was working with Bridget in the pottery shed, Ben and Hannah were drawing pictures with Viv in the kitchen in the farmhouse and John was up on the farmhouse roof. 'Hi, Charlie,' he called as I went by. 'Pass me up that piece of wood, will you?' I climbed half-way up the ladder with the length of wood, handed it up to John, who nodded his thanks, and then set off up the track, keen to escape before someone gave me another job to do.

I was still at the bottom end of the tunnel of trees when suddenly I became aware that something or someone was watching me. Whatever it was, it was among the trees at the far end of the tunnel. I was sure there was a face, a person who was peering at me. I stopped in my tracks and froze with fear. Now I felt sure I could see a pale-faced man, someone tall and thin and leery. I suppose he was about fifty metres away but I could see his expression clearly. It imprinted itself on my brain.

It was obvious that the man was lurking, not walking. For some reason or other, I felt sure he was spying because as soon as he saw that he'd been seen, he jerked back into the bushes on the left-hand side of the track. Everything went quiet, as if he hadn't been there at all. But then a loud squawking came from the trees where I'd seen him. A second later, there was a panicky flapping of wings as something flew up through the branches. I realised that the strange-looking guy must have disturbed a bird that was perched there, and that's when I knew for certain that I wasn't making him up.

It gave me a terrible fright. I wondered who the man could be and what he was looking for and why he was there in our lane. If he was above-board, I reckoned he would have spoken to me and not jumped back into the bushes. I was sure it was something suspicious that made him hide.

Of course, sorry to say, I didn't have the nerve to go up there and confront him. I just turned and pelted back down the lane, through the gate into Greenland. Mollie came rushing towards me from the farmhouse steps where she'd been sleeping in the sun. She started barking round my ankles as if she knew something was wrong. Then Matthew came out of the farmhouse to see what was going on. He took one look at me and said, 'You haven't been up on the road, have you?' 'No,' I replied, which was true in a way. But it wasn't the whole truth either.

The man was my first omen that something bad was going to happen. That night, I couldn't stop thinking about him. Lying under my duvet in the yurt, staring at the cloths hanging down round my bed, I began seeing evil faces peeping out of the patterns. One had a mouth with a very long tongue. Another had one eye staring out of its forehead. I turned over so that my face was on the pillow and squeezed my eyes closed in order to keep the faces away. Then I remembered something else strange that I'd hardly bothered about at the time.

I told you that I'd already been up to the junction once before on my own. Well, I'd gone quite a way along the road that time and was beginning to think that I ought to turn back when this old guy came cycling towards me.

'Lost your way?' the old guy asked, wobbling on his

bike as he came nearer. Then he stopped and spoke to me again. He had a gravelly voice and a very Welsh accent and at first I didn't understand what he said. 'Lost your way?' he said again, but not really looking in my direction.

'No, I'm fine,' I said. 'Just exploring.'

The old man glanced quickly across at me, but as if he didn't exactly want to see me. Then he asked me another question. 'Living round these parts are you?' he said in his rough, squeaky voice.

'Not really,' I answered. 'Just visiting.'

I still don't know why I said it. Just shy, I suppose, and I definitely didn't want to get into a conversation. I didn't want to have to talk about Greenland. Anyway, the old man looked like he was preparing to go on his way. 'Oh, so you're all right then?' he said, again not looking at me but with the same kind of questioning sound in his voice as that waitress had had in the café where Dad and I stopped on our way to Greenland. 'Not lost . . . not lost . . .?' Then he pushed off with his left foot and sat back on his saddle and wobbled off along the road towards the place where our lane came up and joined it. I watched him go but of course I was too far away to know if he carried straight on or actually turned down our track. When I went back, I felt nervous in case I saw him again, but I didn't. Nothing much had happened. It was just an old man going past on his bike. But remembering him makes me feel weird even now, especially in the light of what happened later.

Another thing I recall, looking back, was that when

things started going wrong, it was unusually hot for that time of the year. It was already October. Everyone noticed how steamy it was. 'Hot for the start of October,' Dad would comment at least three times a day. We were talking about global warming all the time. When we were all in the farmhouse eating supper together, Jeremy would remind us that without experimental projects like ours, people were never going to learn to live without using up the earth's natural resources. He would talk about sustainable ways of providing light and power and ways of growing things that don't wreck the planet. And he would always end with the same remark: 'So what we're doing is very important!'

In my mind, I realise now, the funny weather got all mixed up with my spooky feeling of people spying on us, wanting to find out our secrets.

After seeing the thin man looking out of the bushes, I felt too nervous to go up the lane out of Greenland again. I didn't dare, not on my own, and for some reason or other I didn't want to talk about him either. So I didn't say anything to anyone about him. Instead, I went back to exploring our valley from the inside. I started trying to discover a way up the steep wooded hillside that's still part of our land on the other side of our little river.

The first thing I managed was crossing the river just down from the farmhouse. Because the river separates the big field where we live and grow our fruit trees from the hillside the other side, no one had bothered about it very much as yet. We had plenty to do already.

To get across the river, I made stepping stones by moving some rocks into the flow of the water. Then I started exploring the part of the woods that reaches down to the side of the river and I soon found a brilliant place for a den, a hollow tree with one branch growing down low almost parallel with the ground. The idea of the den soon took all my attention. First I created a side for the den by making a framework from twigs. I made uprights long enough so that they'd reach up to the branch when their ends were stuck in the ground, then when the framework was finished, I wove creepers in and out of the gaps.

While I was constructing this first wall for the den, I was thinking about the overall shape I wanted. I propped smaller branches against the main branch to provide a kind of tent shape. Then I set about creating the other walls of the den in a similar way.

It was a stop and start job, though. You get bored doing a task like that on your own. Several times, instead of working on the den, I took time to start exploring the hillside. Unfortunately, getting away from Matthew wasn't always easy. He usually wanted to kick a ball about for an hour or two each afternoon and often I agreed to play with him so he wouldn't think I was always going off by myself. I suppose I also wanted to head him off from asking me about my project. Amy and Ben and Hannah sometimes wanted to join in the football too, and I'll say one thing for Amy: she's really good. But once or twice a week I did manage to get away on my own. I just said I had to get on with my project and, amazingly, they never followed.

I could see that the woods up the hillside above my den were thickset as far as I could see. But I wanted to know what they were like higher up again and what happened at the top of the hill. Dad and Jeremy had recently begun talking about making a start on managing the woodlands on this side of Greenland. Up till now, when they'd had time, they'd been working on the woods on the same side as the road. Now even though they were already very busy, what with all the building and the amount of time Jeremy was away giving lectures, it looked like they might soon begin coppicing the trees over this side. I wanted to finish my exploring before then.

10

It was another very hot day, one Wednesday in October. Mum had written to say sorry, but because work was busy, she wouldn't be able to come and visit till early in November. A few days later, Dad was going away on a course, something to do with managing wood that meant he would be gone for two weeks, somewhere the other side of London. He was getting his tools and papers ready, and he wasn't in a very good mood. Our old van had started going wrong and he didn't trust it to get to London. So he was going to have to go on the train, and that meant he would have to leave most of his tools behind because they'd be too heavy. 'Trust the old van to go wrong right now,' he moaned. It seemed like a good idea to get out of the way and do some exploring.

Several times before, I'd tried getting up the hillside beyond my den but the ground was extremely steep in places and the trees were very dense. This time, I was determined to make it to the top.

Getting away from Matthew wasn't easy that afternoon. Yet again he wanted to play football in between helping on Greg and Nuala's house. Amy insisted on playing too, though I suspected she was deliberately being awkward. 'Oh come on,' she said. 'Stop thinking that football is only for boys. I can be just as good as you.' After only a short time, Ben and Hannah came running over. We let them join in, but of course it changed things and soon everyone got tired and wandered off to do other things, so I was able to escape.

It was hard work climbing the hillside. Not far past my den, the woods got even thicker and the hillside itself became very steep. Every time I got to an extra steep bit, I remembered all over again why I'd found it tough-going before. In many of these places the ground was also covered with a thick prickly undergrowth of brambles and ferns. It took a long time to find a way through. But when I finally got within sight of the top of the hill, it was fantastic. Like coming out into the air after you've been underground.

It was when I reached the top that I first saw the cottage. As I came up through the last part of the woods, the trees grew much more sparsely. Then I was running as the view opened up into a huge green field and a wide blue sky. I started jumping up and down and shouting, not to anyone or anything, just to the air I suppose, and then I remember stopping. There it was, at the top of the field to my right – the little whitewashed cottage, huddled below the brow of the hillside; the place I first saw Megan.

Leading up to the cottage was that gravel path. I also noticed that where the gravel started were two old gateposts. The post on the right-hand side was broken. Even from where I was standing, I could see it was crumbling away. What I couldn't see from that position was any sign of a gate – although the next time I came there, I saw it was lying on the ground, gradually rotting away in the weather.

I'd been staring up at the cottage, wondering whether maybe an old, old man or woman lived there, never expecting a girl. And then the front door opened.

My second visit was a few days later, on a Saturday afternoon. Jeremy was away giving one of his lectures, John had gone to Carmarthen to take Dad to the station so he could catch the train and Matthew had gone with them. So I had no one to muck about with. Viv and Bridget were working on the farmhouse and taking turns to look after the twins. Irina had started preparing one of her feasts for our supper and I was helping.

While she was cooking, Irina started talking about her plans. She said that in about a week she would also be going away. 'Just for a V-E-R-R-Y few days, my D-A-R-R-R-LING. To see some O-T-H-E-R friends that are living in A-N-O-T-H-E-R part of Wales. And you must T-RRR-U-S-T me! You K-N-O-W I'll return.

46

I'll be back L-O-N-G before Nuala's baby arrives. Then I will be H-E-R-E again and we will carry on our lessons.'

Amy was hanging around in the kitchen all this while. In the end, I couldn't wait to get out. I felt cross with Irina because she would be going away and with Dad for going away already and I was mad at Amy too for staying.

As I made my way up through the woodlands, I was able to follow the path I'd beaten out before. I even noticed some of my own footprints still embedded in the muddiest places, and skid marks where I'd slipped.

This time when I reached the top of the hill, I glanced carefully around before coming out from the trees. It was getting towards the end of the afternoon but the light was still good. I looked up the field towards the cottage and realised that if I made my way up through the trees to my right, I could get level with the cottage without going out in the open.

Then I noticed that there was actually a kind of hedge which stretched from the edge of the forest and went all the way along behind the cottage. If I could get up to where this hedge began, I could probably scout along behind it without any risk of being seen. I had no way of knowing if the girl – or anyone else – lived in the cottage, but this time I had to be extremely careful. I definitely didn't want to be spotted again.

First I took a good look all round me. From somewhere out of sight down the hill to my left, a curl of smoke rose high in the air. It didn't look like the smoke from a bonfire and it was almost directly in line with the track that ran down the hillside away from the cottage. I decided it must be coming from a farmhouse. Otherwise there was no evidence of a soul, and there was no sound either except for the meh-ing of sheep.

I put my plan into action. Scrambling through ferns, I worked my way through the woods till I came up level with the cottage. Now I could see it would be easy to get behind the hedge which I hoped would give me cover. Just one more bush to negotiate before I was crouching down behind the hedge, which I now saw was really an overgrown wall, probably a boundary wall. It provided exactly the protection I needed. Crouching down and running alongside it, I was almost immediately behind the cottage.

The first thing I studied when I peered over the wall was the shed that leaned against the pine end of the cottage. The door of the shed was not properly shut, I could see it moving back and fore in the breeze. The left-hand section of the cottage from where I was looking was built out a bit at the back. In this wider section, there was a small square window, its frame in poor condition. I decided to try climbing over the wall so I could take a look through the glass. My heart pounding a bit, I negotiated the wall, then leapt across the rough patch of ground between it and the cottage. Suddenly I heard the call of a buzzard. I looked up quickly to try and spot it. But although I kept on searching, sweeping my eyes from side to side, I couldn't locate it. It kept on calling like a little hurt kitten. Hesitating, I slowly straightened up from my crouching position under the window and looked in.

What I saw was a very small kitchen. Opposite the window was a closed door that obviously led into the main part of the cottage. Hanging from a hook on the back of the door was something that looked like an apron. It might have been bright blue at one time but now it was bleached of colour. Apart from that, there was nothing except for a square stone sink and a metal draining-board to one side of the room and on the other, an old wooden table covered with a piece of worn red lino.

To see any more, I needed to get to the other window that I'd spotted in the back wall of the cottage. But a spiky-looking thorn bush was in the way. The bush was actually growing out of the wall I'd jumped over and it leaned towards the cottage, filling up all the space between where I was standing and the other window further along. One branch almost touched the glass of the window, others reached out towards it. I wouldn't be able to get close enough to take a look through. Instead I jumped back over the boundary wall and after I'd passed the thorn bush, jumped down again beside the far wall of the cottage.

Slowly and carefully I went round the end wall of the cottage. Just past the corner was a wooden door, one of those that are made in two parts which you can open separately if you want to. It was solid shut. I crouched down and crept along towards the front door but stopped underneath the window to the left of the door.

It was too dark inside for me to see very much, but at least I was now peering into the main part of the

49

cottage. I managed to make out some kind of table in the middle of the room and saw that something like an empty sack was lying on top of it. Beyond it everything was in deep shadow.

Crouching again and keeping my head down, I ran swiftly past the front doorway till I came to the window the other side of the door. Before attempting to go into the cottage, I wanted to take another look inside just in case I could make out anything else. I wasn't much wiser even then, other than that from this side I could see, near the back of the room, something like a curtain hanging down from the ceiling. It seemed a bit of an odd place to put one but at least the curtain didn't move and, after a couple of minutes, I felt fairly sure that the cottage was empty.

11

Just in case, I knocked on the door. And waited. I couldn't help starting to giggle at the thought of what I was doing. The girl I'd seen had had a shock when she saw me by the trees a few days before. What if she answered the door today and it turned out she lived there? And what if it turned out she lived there all on her own?

But of course there was no answer. Taking hold of the door knob, I turned it quickly and gave the door a shove. It groaned but didn't open. I shoved it again. It really was stiff. Then suddenly it gave way and I was tumbling inside. I slammed the door shut behind me.

Inside was more like a storehouse than a place for living in. Basically there was one big low room with no ceiling. Above the rafters you could see the slates of the roof. The walls of the room had once been whitewashed, but now they were grimy and covered in cobwebs. Round the fireplace they were black with soot.

The fireplace was massive, a bit like the one we've got down in Greenland. Viv calls ours the range. This one was slightly smaller with a place for an open fire. I could see ashes in the grate, and some half-burned bits of paper. These looked as if they'd only recently been burnt and there was still a sour smell of burning when you got near them. An old kettle hung over the open grate on a chain that came down from the ceiling. The hook that the kettle hung on was also black and thick with soot.

The fireplace was in the left hand wall of the cottage. Before it was another open doorway that led into something like a storehouse. When I went and peered in, I saw a funny arrangement of low stone walls inside. I couldn't think what they might be until I remembered a little shelter we'd been making ready for keeping some goats down at Greenland. Maybe this was a place where you put your animals in the wintertime. When I noticed the two-part wooden door, which I'd already seen from the outside, I decided I was probably right.

But the thing that really caught my attention was towards the back of the main room of the cottage. Making a kind of private area inside the room was a funny arrangement of cloths, like a kind of tent. The cloths hung down from the rafters and they stretched across most of the back wall of the cottage. To the right of them was a door which I thought must be the way into the kitchen that I'd seen from the outside. When I opened the door, I not only saw it, I smelled it. The tiny little room was musty with a tinge of sour milk.

The cloths hanging down from the rafters were old red curtains. They were pinned over pieces of rope that were cleverly strung across the rafters so that the cloths would make their own separate space. It reminded me of where I sleep in Greenland and although I was positive there was no one there, I felt terribly nervous when I took hold of one of the curtains, drew it back and looked inside.

Inside was like a little house with a bed, a table and an old wooden chair. There were magazines on the table. I picked them up – *Girl Plus, 17*. They must be the girl's.

Yet the place didn't look comfy enough to live in, not properly. The bed was covered with a faded pink candlewick bedspread, and when I lifted the cover to look underneath, I could see there was only one blanket. Some cushions were piled at the end of the bed. I don't know if they were supposed to act as pillows, but they were very thin and lumpy. Feathers leaked from the side of one of them. A candleholder on the table looked tatty and worn; its white enamel was mostly chipped off. But there was the stump of a candle in the holder and the grease that had dropped from it was fresh, no dust on it at all.

I was in the middle of quizzing about like this, using my powers of detection, when I heard the front door push open. First came the sound of wood scraping against the stone floor. Then the sound of the door banging against the wall as it swung open. I jumped back onto the edge of the bed, dropping the curtain behind me. At the same moment, I heard an intake of breath and footsteps coming towards me.

'I thought it would be you!' The girl had come straight to the curtains and lifted back one edge. She stood there holding the material, astonished. 'I thought I'd find you here. I thought I'd find you up here,' she repeated. She didn't look angry or afraid – just surprised.

She spoke with a lot of emphasis. 'But I didn't think you'd have the cheek to actually come in the cottage!'

Her voice went up and down like singing and I couldn't take in what she was saying at first because it sounded so different from people in London or Greenland. It sounded a lot more emotional and kind of upset.

'Aren't you going to say nothing at all?' she said. I didn't reply. Something was sticking into my thigh from the mattress and I was feeling around under me to see what it was. When I stayed silent, she suddenly looked really fed-up. She shrugged her shoulders as if she couldn't believe it.

'You got to say *something*, don't you see? You were up here the other day, and I thought to myself you'd be back. Only I didn't think you'd come right on into the cottage. An' now you have done, you got to say *something*.'

I knew I was beaten. After another long pause I muttered, 'Sorry.'

Whatever was sticking into the top of my leg from the mattress was prickly like a hedgehog, and it hurt.

'Sorry,' I said again. 'I didn't mean to be rude, only I just wondered if anyone lived here. So I thought I'd come and find out.'

All the time I was speaking, I was feeling around beneath my knees. In the end, I had to look down to see what exactly was pricking my leg. As I pulled it out from under me, I saw it was something blue and plastic and bristly.

'It's a hairbrush,' I cried. Then, holding out the brush or what was left of it towards the girl, I added, 'But it's got no handle.' Feeling under the mattress again to see if the handle was there, I added, 'I hope it wasn't me that broke it. And if it was me, I'm ever so sorry.'

Suddenly she was laughing. 'Don't be daft! It's been broken for ages. I put it there for a joke last time me and my friends were up here.'

Then she added, ''Scuse me for laughin'. But you did look ever so funny just now, before you found it. You were jigglin' about like you had ants in your pants.'

'Well, it was prickly, wasn't it?' I said a bit sharply.

'That's how it was meant to be, stupid,' she answered.

And that's when I realised we'd started being friends. Just like that.

12

Megan's got an older sister called Catrin who absolutely loves pop music. In fact, one of the first things Megan told me that first day was that Catrin had tickets for the Furries in Cardiff in a couple of weeks' time.

'Wow!' I said, a bit sarcastic. 'What are the Furries when they're at home?'

'You never heard of Super Furry Animals?' Megan couldn't believe it. You could see her thinking I had a lot to learn.

Her father is a farmer called Mr Evans and her mother helps on the farm. Her mother's also got a part-time job, demonstrating milking equipment for Milk Marque, some company that deals with cows' milk.

Megan likes *Neighbours* and *Pobl y Cwm*.

'Don't suppose you've heard of them either?' she asked me, all hoity-toity. When I said, 'No, not that last one you said,' she explained about having soaps in Welsh.

'And *Pobl y Cwm*'s the best,' she said. 'It means the People of the Valley.'

It turned out Megan is nearly the same age as me – eleven at that time, twelve by today.

'Next September,' she said, 'I'll be goin' to Town School.'

I asked her where her new school would be, and she said it would be the secondary school in Llandysul. She'd be travelling by bus from the end of their lane.

Megan also told me about the cottage. She said the people that used to live there were an ancient old couple who helped her father on the farm. When they'd died a few years back, Megan's father didn't want to rent it to anyone else. But he didn't want to pull it down either. So it just stayed there, empty, until Megan had the idea of having a den.

Because Megan told me so much about herself, I told her quite a lot about myself too except that, even before I really got started, I had to tell her it was kind of secret. She couldn't tell anyone else.

'Why not?' she asked me, looking shocked.

So I had to explain about Greenland and what we were trying to do there and why. She nodded a lot as I was speaking and said they'd been doing about the environment at school and she thought it was very important.

She asked me if we were like eco-warriors. So we talked a bit about the campaign that was going on at that time to stop a road by-pass being built near some town in the south of England. At Greenland, we used to talk about this campaign a lot. Greg and Nuala knew one of the blokes that had dug himself a tunnel under the ground so he could live there and try and keep the bulldozers away. When anyone from Greenland went to town and brought back a paper, we'd look for the latest press stories about him. I also told Megan some things Jeremy had said about similar campaigns in other parts of the world like Canada and India.

Megan and I talked to each other for what seemed like hours, and afterwards it seemed obvious that we would be seeing each other again. We arranged to meet at the top of the forest the next afternoon.

She was swinging on the branch of a half-fallen tree when I came up through the woods.

'Why does it matter to you all, bein' so secret?' She asked this question almost as soon as I got there.

I tried going over it all again about the building experiments we were doing at Greenland and why they were important.

'So why exactly can't you be telling? Don't people need to know about it?'

First I went over the ecology side about working out how to make buildings without using materials that use up the earth's resources. I said some of the things Dad would have said about respecting the earth and putting stuff back – like through waste-recycling, energy conservation and all that stuff. Then I went on to tell her about us, the people that live in Greenland, especially us kids: me, Amy, Matthew and the twins. She was especially interested about Amy and Matthew not being brother and sister and when I said that Amy was grumpy, she sounded very sympathetic. 'Perhaps she misses her Mum,' she said, tipping her head to one side. Maybe that was right. But as I told Megan, Bridget was always really nice to Amy, and anyway in Greenland it's as if all the kids have got lots of parents – and teachers, in a way.

'If outside people knew about us being there, they'd probably come poking their nose in and we'd probably end up having to go to school.'

'And what'd be wrong with that?' Megan tipped her head to the side as she had before. 'School's all right, isn't it? At least you get friends and somethin' to do every day. And then you get to go on trips, be in plays and all that sort of stuff.'

I answered the best way I could. I know some of what I said were ideas I'd picked up from the grown-ups at Greenland. But I really thought they were true as well. I did like the way of learning we had, following my nose, not always having to do things like putting your name on the top of the paper or standing in line to go back in the classroom. I admitted that sometimes I did feel lonely but pretended I didn't really mind.

Megan didn't sound completely convinced, but I could see she was prepared to think about it and that she partly understood what I was talking about. And I knew I could trust her.

So that's why I agreed when she asked me if I'd like to go to her house for tea a couple of days later, on Tuesday. She said at once that there wouldn't be anyone at home when I came, no one except us, that is.

'Won't you be at school?' I asked.

'Next week is half-term, dumbo,' Megan said. 'But p'raps you don't know those kind of things anymore, do you? I don't s'pose it affects you.'

13

I spent most of Monday afternoon making Megan a present. It was a ladder for her gerbil-cage. She'd told me about her gerbils, the second time we met. I've always wished I could have some. Hers sounded like really nice pets. She said she had two. One of them was

58

black and one was white and she'd called them Nos and Dydd, which is the Welsh for night and day.

By the time I started on the gerbil-ladder, I was glad to have something practical to do. The atmosphere in Greenland had started getting weird.

It all began that Monday morning when John came back from collecting the post in Carmarthen.

Irina and I were in the farmhouse having one of our French conversations. Amy and Matthew had been with us for the first part. Then they had gone off to do something else and Irina was in the middle of explaining about the importance of A-R-R-T and about some painters who had lived in Paris. This was typical of Irina's lessons. She would usually get into some kind of dramatic story. It could be the story of a musician or a painter or a scientist or an explorer. Sometimes she'd pretend to be the person, whoever it was she was talking about. Then after telling me a bit about her life as this person, I would have to interview her – in French, of course. I'd have to think up all kinds of questions such as what kind of music she wrote or what sort of science she preferred to do, where she lived and who she lived with, what she ate, if she was rich or poor. She always made the answers very dramatic and I always felt like I was really there with the person we were talking about.

Then sometimes Irina would suddenly switch, and I had to be the person who was being interviewed. I'd already decided that next time it was my turn to do this, I'd be a very successful painter with rich people buying my paintings and loads of beautiful girls all wanting to go out with me. But I didn't get the chance this time. Instead, Irina suddenly got onto the subject of a painter she liked called Chagall. She told me he'd grown up in Russia and afterwards went to live in France and I could see at once why Irina liked him. He was Russian and wonderful AND he had a weird sense of humour.

Irina told me a story of when Chagall first lived in Paris. For a few years, she said, he was very very poor: 'NO MORE TO EET ZAN A CRRUST OF BREAD!' I wondered how one crust could have lasted so long. But Irina was already into the next part of the story, saying that Chagall eventually managed to find someone rich who was interested in putting his paintings into an exhibition. The only trouble was that it was going to be in Germany. So after choosing some of his paintings and sending them off, Chagall decided to go too, so he could be there when it happened. Before he left, he stacked all the rest of his paintings in the little shed in Paris which he used as his studio. Then he put a big padlock on the door and locked it up. 'AU R-R-REVOIR,' said Irina, pretending to be Chagall and blowing a stylish kiss in the air. 'I'LL BE BACK ZOON.'

But he wasn't. Irina said that, after Germany, Chagall decided to make a trip back to Russia so he could visit his parents and his Russian girlfriend. He only meant to be there a short while but while he was there, the First World War started. So Chagall wasn't allowed to leave Russia. 'ZE FIGHTING . . . ZE ZUFFERING . . . NO PERMISSION FOR TRAVEL . . .'

Nine years went by. Then guess what happened? On the day Chagall finally got back to Paris, he went

60

straight to the shed where he'd left his paintings. But the place was not even locked. Instead the door was wide open and inside was a man sitting on a chair in front of an easel with a paint brush in one hand and a palette on the other. Chagall had never seen this man before but he looked as if he owned the place. He burst in and looked round the walls, searching for his paintings. None of the paintings that were there were his. 'They were R-R-RUBBISH!' said Irina. 'SOMEONE ELZES R-R-R-RUBBISH!' So that's when Chagall discovered that his friends had decided he must be dead. They thought he was never coming back. So they'd sold his paintings and found someone else to rent his studio.

Irina had just finished this story when she remembered she had a book about Chagall at the bottom of her trunk. She had brought this trunk with her to Greenland and she kept it beside her bed in our yurt. It contained an amazing selection of books and every now and again she would open it with a flourish as if there was magic inside, which in a way there was. 'W-A-I-T!' said Irina, rushing out of the kitchen. When she came back, she had a colourful art book in her hand. She started showing me the pictures. They were zany. Some had people floating in the sky like clouds. Lots had a clock or a violin, or maybe a chicken or a donkey. Or a ladder. I liked the ladders and they're what made me think of making a gerbil-ladder for Megan.

A few days before, I'd found some bits of a broken-up wooden bird-cage in an old rubbish heap at the back of the farmhouse. As I looked at Chagall's pictures, I thought I could use the pieces of bird-cage to make a double-sided gerbil-ladder: the gerbils could climb up one side and slide down the other. I was thinking about how I'd construct it when John suddenly appeared in the doorway of the kitchen where Irina and I were sitting. He was wearing his usual dungarees and check shirt. He had a bundle of letters in his hand and he looked extremely glum.

'Vot's R-R-R-ong?' Irina said to John at once. 'Some-zing AWFUL in the letters?' John didn't respond to the question. He just shrugged his shoulders and said, 'Where's Viv?' but it was obvious something was the matter. 'VIV? Doing zum W-A-SHING, NO?' Irina replied and John quickly retreated out of the door. Irina shrugged and made one of her funny faces and we carried on looking at the books on the table until Irina suddenly said, 'E-E-E-NOUGH! That's enough for T-O-O-DAY. Now what's going to be NEXT?' I said I'd got an idea: I was going to try making something creative.

As I went round the back of the farmhouse, I saw that John and Viv were standing outside the wash-house. They were obviously involved in a serious conversation. Viv was standing close to John, one minute peering at him like she didn't know what to think, the next minute turning towards the clothes-line to peg something on the line, then turning back towards John once more. She looked very concerned and John was hunched over, both hands deep in his dungaree pockets, his hair flopping over his forehead. He happened to look up as I went by and he nodded at me briefly. But when I looked back, a few seconds later, he was staring down at the ground again and I could see that he and Viv were once more deep in conversation.

I wondered what was so important. Then I got distracted, thinking the shirts that Viv had put on the line reminded me of Chagall's pictures. Billowing on the line, they looked as if they were floating and there were so many different colours – Irina's reds and purples, John's checked blues and browns, and the twins' minuscule shirts in bright reds and yellows. My T-shirts were mostly white with pictures on them. With the air filling them out, they looked like sails on ships sailing over the seas.

When lunch-time came, it was spinach soup and walnut bread. I really liked that walnut bread. Irina kept passing me more but Viv didn't even seem to notice how much I was eating. Normally she would have said something nice because she liked it when I enjoyed her food. But on this occasion, she hardly said anything at all to me or Matthew or Amy or Bridget. In between helping Ben and Hannah, she looked as if her mind was on something else. For once, John wasn't with us: he'd taken a sandwich over to Greg and Nuala's house.

After lunch, I couldn't wait to get back to my gerbil-ladder except that, before I managed to get out of the kitchen, Viv asked me if I wanted to help her make pastry. Again! I'd helped with pastry only two days before. This time it was for a pie for supper. Hannah sat under the table as we started working. I could hear her counting – mostly up to three and starting over.

Viv began collecting the ingredients for the pastry and I started weighing them out. Viv had become chatty again – she was talking about some game that Ben had been playing – and I thought she seemed back to her usual self. Then out of the blue, in a different tone of voice, she asked me what Irina and I had been working on that morning. I started telling her about Chagall but seconds later, just as I started rolling out the pastry, she changed the subject again. 'Oh, and Charlie, be careful, won't you?' Now she sounded quite strained. 'I mean, you know what we're all trying to do here. It's important to all of us. So try keeping away from the road at the top of the lane. We don't want anyone asking questions or coming down here to poke around. Not now. Not yet.'

I couldn't ever remember Viv giving me that kind of talking-to before. She is usually so sweet-tempered, so keen to see everyone's point of view. Besides, being in Greenland had always felt like being part of a team. Except when Jeremy got carried away, going on about his ideas, the grown-ups always drew me in to the conversation. But this was new: speaking as if there were *rules*.

As soon as I managed to get away from Viv and the baking, I went over to the yurt to fetch the bits of old bird-cage. I sat down on my bed and started to study the pieces. Partly I just wanted to be on my own to think. And I really did want to work out my idea for Megan's present. One piece of bird-cage, I decided, could be for the ladder section, but some of its horizontal bars were missing. I'd have to fill in the gaps with bits from one of the sections I wasn't going to need. Another smooth piece of wood could be for the slide, and I already had visions of the gerbils swooshing down it, but I realised that I'd have to find a way to join it to the ladder section.

I took the bits and pieces across to the carpentry shed, which is in one of the outbuildings next to Bridget's pottery room. It's a place where John spends a lot of his time and I always like the smell from the heaps of sawdust and the long thin curls that come off the wood when it's being planed to smoothe it. Besides, John is quiet, he doesn't ask questions and it's nice being in there when he is hard at work. I wondered if he'd be there that afternoon.

On my way, I popped in to see Bridget. She'd gone back to her pottery straight after lunch to finish a couple of pots for the special bonfire firing. She was rubbing them over with a pebble, making them smooth and shiny. Ben was with her, chattering away. He was making some animals out of the clay. 'See – dinosaur,' he said, then immediately squashed what he'd made in his hands and started all over again.

'Just on my way to do some woodwork,' I called out, wondering if Bridget knew if something was wrong and whether she'd say anything about it. She didn't. She just looked up and grinned at me through her whacky red specs and went back to rubbing her pots and asking Ben about dinosaurs.

The carpentry shed was empty and all the time I was working on my gerbil-ladder, I kept on thinking about what had happened that morning. Why had John looked so worried? Why did Viv say those things about not talking to anyone on the road? Somehow I couldn't help linking what she'd said to that creep I'd seen in the lane. I even wondered whether to keep my promise to go to tea with Megan the next day. That would really be breaking the rules and what would happen if anyone found out?

Over supper I could hardly speak. Irina and Bridget both noticed how quiet I was. But when Irina asked me later if anything was the matter, I didn't tell her what it was. I knew she was going to be leaving to visit her friends in two days' time and I didn't want to bother her. I just went to bed and tried to sleep.

14

In the morning, all of us kids were excited. This was the day we were going to do our firing experiment with Bridget. Bridget usually uses a wood-fired kiln for cooking her pots but today we were going to put the pots in a special pit outside.

The day before, Matthew and Amy and I had dug the pit and prepared big piles of different size pieces of wood. We'd also fetched some binfuls of sawdust from the carpentry shed. Now we started by collecting the pots we'd been making from Bridget's pottery shed where she'd been drying them out. We laid them carefully beside the pit until all of them were stacked there. I had one special pot I wanted to fire. This was a pot with two ears that I'd pinched out of the clay, one on each side of the pot. I was really keen to see how it would turn out. I also had a couple of plain little bowls, but I didn't much care about them. Ben and Hannah had some funny lumpy little pots in the shape of different creatures such as a mouse, some cats, a monkey and a pig. Matthew had a couple of boxes that he'd carefully constructed from slabs of clay and Amy, like me, had one special pot that I was convinced she had copied from mine, though she pretended she hadn't. As well as two ears, her pot also had eyes and a nose.

After laying our pots in the bottom of the pit, with sawdust packed around them, we began to cover them up, first with small stuff like more leaves and sawdust, then with bits and pieces from the woodshed, then with sticks and branches. 'It's going to be fun to see what colours they come out,' said Bridget. 'That's if they hold together! I don't know if this experiment is going to work. But if they do come out whole, they could be a very nice mixture of browns and blacks, maybe even some silver, we'll see.'

When the whole thing was mounded over, Bridget set light to it. Ben and Hannah both wanted to be the ones to do the lighting, but Bridget said, 'No, fire is very strong. It can turn nasty. You have to be careful.'

The fire began slowly, smouldering at first because of some damp leaves we'd put on the top. Then flames began licking round the far edge. Soon it was ablaze and we had to stand back. Then, as it gradually settled, coils of smoke began rising high in the air. I love that smell. I stood away where it wasn't too hot and watched. Bridget had her work cut out to keep Hannah away from the mound. Ben just stood staring in awe at the fire. But Hannah had found a long stick somewhere and you could see that what she wanted to do was to poke it about in the fire. 'No, Hannah, no,' Bridget told her. 'We must leave the fire to do its work. It doesn't like to be disturbed.'

'When can we get them out?' Hannah asked for about the twentieth time. She looked hilarious with smudges of ash all over her face, chin and neck. Bridget replied, 'Not for a long time yet. First the fire has to burn down until all that's left is ashes. Then we have to let it cool and after that, we can dig out our pots and see what's happened to them. It will be exciting. Tomorrow morning after breakfast, we'll come over and do it.' 'No, now,' shouted Hannah, jumping up and down and yelling loudly, 'Now, now, now,' until Matthew grabbed her and started swinging her round to take her mind off the subject.

Like Hannah, I too was feeling impatient, but for different reasons. I wanted to get going and first there had to be lunch. We had ours early, Bridget and us kids, because we were so hungry after doing the fire. We ate what was left of the spinach soup and all the remains of the pie from supper. When we'd finished, Bridget collected the plates and went in to the scullery to start on the washing-up.

'OK, see you lot later,' I said to the others as I got up from the table.

'Where are you going?' Hannah asked at once. 'Can't you come and play with me?'

'Not this afternoon,' I said. 'I want to get on with my mapping.'

I took the bowls into the scullery and when I told Bridget what I was going to do, she gave me an odd sort of look. 'Charlie,' she said, 'I've been meaning to ask you how you're getting on with your project – and with everything really. I was wondering if it's all starting to fit together for you at Greenland – all of us and what you're doing.'

'It's OK,' I replied. 'It's fine.'

I could tell she'd have liked to ask me more. But she didn't quiz me. She says things carefully, Bridget does, so you don't have to say things in return if you don't want to. I definitely didn't feel like talking at that moment. For one thing, Amy was hanging about in the doorway, and I couldn't stand for her to know anything about me that she didn't have to. Then again, I also wanted to get away to meet up with Megan. She'd said tea-time and already it was three o'clock and I still had to get up the hill.

I asked Bridget if I could take a piece of cake for later. 'Of course you can,' she said and when I was cutting it, I made sure it was a big piece, big enough for two.

As I was walking away from the farmhouse to go over to our yurt to fetch my daysack, I passed Jeremy coming from the direction of the roundhouse. It's almost hidden by bushes, so I didn't see him at first. He was striding across to the house, probably to get something for his lunch.

'All right, Charlie?' he said when he saw me. 'How are things going? Sometime soon, you must fill me in on your map-project. I'd like to know how it's going.

And maybe I could show you some plans I've been working on, plans for an Energy Centre? I think you'd be interested.'

'OK,' I replied, 'I'd like to look at the plans. Tonight, maybe?'

Then I went on my way, my daysack bouncing against my back. Inside, in the bottom, was the gerbil-ladder I'd made for Megan. I'd wrapped it in one of my T-shirts and on top, in a paper bag, was the piece of cake I'd brought from the farmhouse. It was going to be my contribution to tea.

Going up the hill, I had to watch my step but when I turned round to look back towards Greenland, I was sure I could see a coil of smoke rising from our pottery fire. I wondered if Megan or her parents would have been able to see any sign of it from the old cottage at the top of their hill.

All the way, I was wondering where exactly Megan was going to meet me. I didn't want to have to go down to the farmhouse before seeing her. What if someone else was there, such as her Mum or her sister Catrin? I didn't know what I would say. I'd just feel a bit of a twit. 'Excuse me, I've come to tea, except I was only expecting to see Megan.' Or maybe I'd have to fake it: 'Excuse me, I'm trying to find Pen-y-Cwm but I think I'm lost. Can you help?'

But it was OK. Megan was waiting where you come out from the woods onto the track across the field. She was doing step-ups against the fallen branch of a tree. She was obviously waiting for me. I felt proud and a bit shy too. This was like having a real friend.

15

We set out down the hillside towards Megan's house. It was a bit further down the hill than I'd expected. But otherwise the house was just as I'd imagined, a big square stone house with a flower garden in the front. To the side was another garden for vegetables. Behind I could see a farmyard and barns.

We went into the house through a side-door that we got to through the vegetable garden. The side-door led into a narrow passage which was loaded up with Wellington boots, garden tools and other sorts of stuff. We went past a room where I could see a huge white freezer just inside the door. Then I nearly tripped over a dog's basket that half filled the passage. I could see boxes of dog-food on the shelves above it, plus packets of toilet-paper piled up in a tower. You name it, you'd surely find it in that passage.

Past the room with the freezer was another door leading into another back room. In this one, I could see a washing-machine with a tumble dryer beside it. Both looked new and gleaming white and that surprised me a bit, after Greenland. It made me think of my mum. This was the kind of equipment she'd said she would never give up.

The kitchen itself was amazing. It was a big cosy-looking room with plenty of space and a huge sofa with soft plumpy cushions that made you want to sit down on them right away.

I looked quickly round the room: there was a large-sized TV with a video-machine, a CD player and a computer. The room was crowded with other things too. I spotted school books, roller skates, nail-varnish, magazines, and something that looked like a half-knitted scarf. Also in the room was a dog. Megan said she was a cross between a Labrador and a golden retriever and I fell in love with her at once. She was fast asleep when we came in, curled up in front of the fireplace, which was one for a real coal fire. The fire wasn't actually lit at the time, but the dog was obviously pretending it was. As we came in to the room, her right ear pricked up and she opened an eye and looked round at the two of us. Then she got to her feet, shook herself all over and – 'Woof! Woof!' – she was suddenly all over Megan. Then Megan introduced me: 'Blodwen, this is my new friend Charlie. Charlie, this is Blodwen, the best dog in the whole wide world.'

Then Blodwen was all over me too, jumping up and licking my hands. I suddenly felt dead envious of the dog, the room, the house, even the washing machine and the TV and the computer. It all looked so normal and friendly.

But then Megan was saying, 'Let's have tea. Or d'you want to look round the house first? I can show you my room if you want – and Catrin's.'

So we ended up going all round the house. The front room downstairs was different from the kitchen. I didn't like it at all. Megan said she didn't either. It had a big square table covered with a thick green cloth, then another lacy cloth on top of that, and a big spiky plant in the middle. Along one wall were bookcases, the kind where the books are closed in behind glass doors. Round the table were six chairs with high wooden backs that looked so uncomfortable you knew that if you sat down on them, you'd just wriggle around till you could get up and leave. On each side of the fireplace was a big leather armchair and in the corner was an enormous grandfather clock with a very solemn tick.

'We got to sit in here to have tea when visitors come,' Megan said with a shiver of disgust. 'Not visitors like you, I don't mean. I mean the minister and people like that.'

'What do you mean, minister?' I asked Megan and she explained that the minister was whoever came to do the service in the chapel they went to on Sundays.

'So you go to a chapel then?' I asked her.

'Yes, chapel – not church!' she answered. 'We're Baptists and we go to Salem up in the village. Catrin's going to be accepted as a member next month.'

Upstairs in Megan's house was a gorgeous bathroom with a carpet on the floor and a shower as well as a bath and a big pile of towels on a chair in the corner. There was an airing cupboard too and, because the door was open, I could see there were lots more towels inside, all in nice colours and fluffy. On the edges of the bath was girl's stuff – bubble bath and shampoo and funny-shaped soaps.

Megan's room was great except that the bottom corner of the bed was covered with soft toys so you could hardly see the bed underneath. But the rest of it was fine and she had lots of things on the walls such as a rack of CDs, posters of pop stars, shelves of books and ornaments. On one wall was a poster of a poem in Welsh.

'What's that poem?' I said to Megan.

'Oh, *Cofio*,' she said, 'it's the poem I'm learning. I've got to recite it in the eisteddfod in the village.'

'What's that?' I asked her and she said an eisteddfod was a whole lot of competitions in singing and dancing and saying poems out loud. 'And what's the poem about?' I asked her. She explained that it was about lots of people who lived a long time ago and how we don't know anything much about them now. I got a strange feeling as she spoke that it sounded like us in Greenland except that we are not in the past. But I felt sure that if we suddenly vanished, no one would know, not for ages.

A few minutes later, I got an even weirder feeling. It was like it was meant to happen. On Megan's table was a scrapbook, a thick one with cream-coloured pages, and it was obvious that Megan had already done a lot of work on it. She'd decorated the front cover with a border of flowers and in the middle of the cover was a label, 'Megan's Special Book'. Megan saw me looking and said I could have a look inside if I wanted. So I opened it and began turning the pages. Nearly at the end, I turned onto something that made my hair prickle.

It was a newspaper cutting and the headline was in big black letters: **SECRET COMMUNITY FOUND IN WELSH WOODS.**

16

I don't know if Megan noticed but as I stood there, my muscles tensed up, I tried to take it in that Greenland had been discovered. Was this the reason why John and Viv had been looking so worried the day before? We were in the papers!

The story occupied two whole pages of the scrapbook and my eyes zoomed up and down and back and fore across the lines, trying to absorb it. There was a big photograph as part of the article. It showed a ruined house only partly visible among lots of trees. I couldn't recognise anything about the building or the surroundings and slowly I began to realise that the story wasn't about Greenland at all.

Megan must have noticed my stunned expression. 'What you looking at?' she asked me.

'This article,' I answered lamely. 'Seems quite strange for someone to actually discover a village no one knew was there.'

'That's what I thought,' Megan replied. 'That's why I cut it out. Sort of goes with that poem I'm learnin', the one I'm doin' in the 'steddfod.'

Megan obviously didn't realise how hard the story had struck me. Or had she? She started giggling and then burst out: 'Bit like you lot down there, isn't it?'

As my eyes focused on what was actually printed, I saw that the date of the newspaper article was several months before, a while before I'd come to Greenland. It was about a ruined village which someone had found in some woods in mid-Wales. No one in the area knew anything about it – who had lived there or when it was built or why it had been abandoned. Local history experts had been trying to solve the mystery, and they thought the village might have been built about a hundred years before by a community of refugees. Yet even that idea didn't quite make sense: the houses were well-built and would have needed money. So even if refugees had built them, they couldn't have been poor people. Another idea was that the people who built them might have been a group of Quakers looking for somewhere they would be safe from people making trouble about their way of life and religion.

I read the story again and again, not straight through but in bits and pieces, trying to take it in. But however hard I tried getting it straight in my head, I couldn't stop thinking that the writer must have got things mixed up, that the community he was talking about was really Greenland. What if the photographer had been somewhere down in my woods, and our secret had been discovered?

'Come on,' I heard Megan saying. 'Haven't you read that thing by now? Let's go down and have tea.'

I still couldn't pull myself away. Even after I managed to close the scrapbook, I stayed stuck to the chair in front of Megan's table. In my mind's eye was Bridget and us kids beside the pit where we'd made our fire to cook our pots, waiting for the ashes to cool and the pots to come out. Then the image blurred for a second and instead I was seeing a group of Quaker people a long time ago, all gathered round an open fire, warming their hands against the cold.

'Come on,' said Megan, pulling at my arm. 'Let's do something else. There's some Welsh cakes we can have for tea.'

I'd never actually eaten Welsh cakes before, though I'd seen them in Carmarthen market, and I must say I've eaten a lot of them since. By now I can make them too. It was Megan's Mum, Mrs Evans, who taught me. Ever since she made friends with us in Greenland, I've even got her private recipe. But now I'm skipping too much and I'll have to go back.

Megan simply couldn't believe that I'd never had Welsh cakes. 'Where've you been?' she asked me. I told her I'd had other sorts of cakes with Welsh names but not these. They were round flat things that looked more like biscuits than cakes, and I thought they were a bit dry at first, but I managed five altogether. They grew on me as I went on.

Then I remembered the cake in my daysack. I fetched the bag and fished out the paper bag with the cake in, and remembered the gerbil ladder I'd made. I reached into the bottom of my daysack for the bundled-up T-shirt I'd wrapped it up in. I felt a bit daft as I got it out of its wrapping. Suddenly it seemed an odd kind of present.

'Guess what this is,' I mumbled, trying to cover my embarrassment.

'Something for gerbils to climb up?' Megan said at once with a cheery smile, as if she was making a guess that couldn't possibly be right.

'And slide down,' I added. 'I thought you might like it for your gerbil cage.'

She leaned over and took it carefully. First she

turned it over in her hand, then she stood it on the table. To my amazement and relief, it didn't fall over.

'Where d'you get it?' she asked me.

'Made it,' I answered, even more embarrassed. 'With some bits of old bird-cage. Anyway, where are your gerbils?'

'Gosh,' she said, 'you haven't seen the gerbils. Come on, they're out the back.'

We went along the passage that led out of the kitchen and into the little room where I'd noticed the freezer. In the corner was a big central heating boiler and on a table next to it was the gerbil cage. One of the gerbils, the black one, was curled up on the upper storey as if she was fast asleep. 'That's Nos,' said Megan, 'because she's black.' Then Megan opened a little door at the bottom and took the other gerbil out from inside. This one was brilliant white.

'This is Dydd,' Megan said, lifting the gerbil's front feet towards me as if the gerbil was saying hello.

After that, Megan put Dydd back in the cage and placed the ladder inside the gerbils' living room on the bottom floor of the cage. She'd hardly taken her hand out when Nos appeared to wake up. She scuttled down the stairs to the living room and waddled straight over to the ladder. Without even pausing, she climbed up the rungs, stopped at the top for a second, then sniffed the air and slid down the other side.

Megan and I started laughing. We laughed even more when Nos went straight back to the ladder, climbed it again and, still without pausing, slid down it like she was in a playground.

Then Dydd seemed to realise something was going on. She stuck her nose out of the bedroom and came over to the bottom of the ladder. But after taking one look at Nos and her antics, with a disgusted look she disappeared back into the bedroom.

This made us laugh even more. After a bit, we went back to the kitchen and ate the cake I'd brought. Then Megan got out a couple of cans of coke and we finished them off straight away.

'We wouldn't be having this down in Greenland,' I said.

'Why not?' she asked.

'Not good for you,' I replied. 'But it's nice though – thanks. I love it.'

Then suddenly it was time to go. As I picked up my daysack ready to say goodbye, the cutting in Megan's scrap-book came back to my mind. I wondered what had happened to the people who had lived in that village, why they'd had to leave. I remembered the Man in the Trees, the man I'd caught spying on our life in Greenland and who'd seen me coming up the lane.

'I'll come with you up to the track,' Megan said, almost as if she'd read my mind.

As we set out, I tried to push the Man in the Trees out of my thoughts. I wondered if I'd ever be coming to her house again. We went up through the field till we came to the track that turned off to the woods. 'Take care,' Megan said in a friendly, concerned sort of way. I knew she could see that I was a bit bothered. 'I'd better be off,' she added, 'so I can tidy up before Mam comes home.'

Then she was gone, running back down the path to her house and waving. 'Be seein' you soon,' she called. But then she stopped and started back up the hill towards me. 'Hey, when exactly?' she added. 'It's school again next week. So I won't have much of a chance. And I've got lots of things on tomorrow and the next day. Tell you what, how about Saturday? After my ballet class, in the afternoon? Up by the old cottage? OK?'

'OK,' I said. Then once again she was off.

I didn't go straight back down to Greenland. I wanted to stay on my own to think. I wanted to try and work out why new information can sometimes produce such a shock in your mind. Because nothing had actually happened, not yet anyway. So far it was all in my head, this idea that secrets can suddenly get discovered.

17

The next day, all hell broke loose. The morning began with Ben and Hannah shaking my feet to wake me up. When I managed to partly open my eyes, I saw they were holding one foot each.

'What's going on?' I asked them. 'Ben . . . Hannah . . . what are you doing?'

'Get up, Charlie! Get up, Charlie. Bridget says the pots are ready. Come on and look, come on.'

I didn't feel like getting up. My sleep in the night

had been full of dreams. One dream still lingered at the back of my mind and all I wanted was to lie quietly in bed and think it out.

A group of people in old-fashioned clothing had been standing around a bonfire which was steadily getting hotter. Each person was holding a saucepan in one hand and a spoon in the other. Suddenly, as if there had been a signal, they all put their saucepans on the fire and began to stir them. There must have been five or six of these people altogether but I couldn't see their faces clearly. They were bent over the saucepans, stirring, stirring. I couldn't see into their saucepans either, but I knew exactly what was inside them: porridge. And I knew it was made from Quaker porridge oats. The porridge was thick and almost ready to eat when something terrible happened.

Down amongst the sticks on the outside edge of the fire, a little furry head popped up. It was a little gerbil. It started climbing towards the top of the fire, hopping from branch to branch and avoiding the parts that were already aflame. Then, very swiftly, it climbed onto one of the pots and hovered for a moment on the edge of the pan before toppling into the porridge. The last I saw of it was its head, bobbing up out of the porridge before one of the people leaned over and, putting his spoon in the saucepan, tossed the gerbil out from the pan.

This whole dream was re-running itself through my head as Ben and Hannah shook my feet. I was desperately trying to remember what had happened afterwards when the twins started pulling my duvet off me, all the time shouting and laughing and tickling my toes. From the other side of the yurt, I could hear Irina: 'HEY! You CHILD-R-R-EN! What are you doing? Is it an earthquake? What E-V-E-R is going on?'

'It's OK, Irina, it's only Ben and Hannah,' I called out loudly. Then, sitting up in bed, I said to the twins, 'All right, all right, I'm coming.' I grabbed my tracksuit bottoms and pulled them on over the shorts that I usually wear in bed. Then I pulled on my jumper and shoved my feet in my trainers.

'OK,' I said. 'Let's go.'

We were half-way out of the yurt when I remembered. This was Wednesday, the day Irina was leaving. She'd be back in a week or so, she had promised. But for now she was going to visit those friends who needed her help for some reason, and Greg and Nuala were going to give her a lift on their way to a Boat Show down in Bristol.

I rushed back into the yurt. 'Irina, Irina, please come back soon,' I called, rushing into Irina's space. She was sitting quietly on her bed, all dressed and ready to go, her enormous brightly-coloured carpet-bag all packed beside her. She must be collecting her thoughts together, I supposed. I gave her an enormous hug and she gave me a big smoodgy kiss on my cheek.

'Now CHARLIE, be yourself,' Irina said as I left. I've thought about that a lot since she said it, wondering exactly what she meant.

'Come on,' I said to Ben and Hannah, who were hopping up and down at the entrance to our yurt. 'Race you to our pot-cooking pit.' As we started running across the field, I heard the rumble of Greg and Nuala's combi van starting up. They usually kept it over by the farmhouse but this time they must have driven it over to where their old bus was parked near their new house.

As the loaded combi lumbered over the field towards us, I could see Nuala sitting in the passenger seat. She was leaning against the window, her long black hair falling over one side of her face, and she looked as sleepy as I felt. When they saw us kids, Greg beeped his horn and grinned, then stopped the van just level with our yurt. 'Hi kids,' he called. 'What ya' all doing this early, hey?' Nuala sat up straight and smiled at us too as Irina appeared from our yurt carrying her bag. She climbed into the combi behind Nuala, and my heart sank as we all waved goodbye. I knew Greg and Nuala would be back by the next Monday or Tuesday. I hoped Irina would return soon after.

As Greg drove out of the Greenland gate, I caught sight of Viv. She was striding across from her yurt to the farmhouse, looking very purposeful. I supposed she was going to make our breakfast. Then it dawned on me that this was probably her second shift. We've got a habit in Greenland that if anyone is leaving, even for a day, someone else in the community will always be sure to be up to give them a meal and see them on their way. She'd probably already been over to the farmhouse once that morning to prepare breakfast for Greg and Nuala and Irina.

The fire in the pit had completely burnt out and you could see that the ashes were cold. I stuck my right foot into them and stirred them around with the toe of my trainer.

'Where's Bridget?' I said to Ben and Hannah. 'We can't dig for the pots without Bridget. And Matthew? Where's Matthew and Amy?'

'Bridget's coming,' Ben replied. 'She's getting dressed.'

I realised the twins must have gone to wake Bridget before they came to wake me. They were really, really excited.

'There she is,' Hannah called out, jumping up and down beside the bed of ashes.

'Bridget, Bridget, we're here . . . we're here. And Charlie.'

Bridget was carrying a couple of big wooden spoons for fishing around in the ashes. Behind her came Matthew, yawning massively, and behind him came Amy looking sulky, like she didn't want to be there – at least, not if I was there too.

Amy and I were both allowed to dig in the ashes. Matthew said he'd have a go later: he was feeling too sleepy to have a go right now.

'Careful now,' Bridget called out as we started. 'We don't want anything broken.'

The first thing to come out was Amy's pot with a face. The pot had gone a blackish brown with a silvery glint round the eyes.

'That's nice, Amy,' Bridget said, and I saw Amy looking secretly pleased. Then – typical of her – she turned away with her pot so none of the rest of us could see it.

The next thing to come out was my pot with the ears. Both of the ears had gone a kind of silvery black, and I thought the whole thing looked brilliant. When I stood it on the grass and stepped back to admire it, it really looked as if it was listening and I decided it was definitely better without a nose or eyes. I laughed and wondered what it could hear.

I was about to find out.

We'd just managed to find the very last pot. It had taken quite a while to locate them all because one or two had shattered in the heat. Matthew's straight-sided boxes had turned out well but some of Ben and Hannah's animals were really tiny, and finding them in the ashes wasn't easy. Just as the last little creature came out, there was the noise of a car on the lane from the road. The noise was coming towards us. My first thought was that it must be Greg and Nuala returning in their combi. But the engine sound wasn't at all the same. I wondered who on earth it could be. When I looked over at Bridget, I could tell she was wondering the same thing.

'Car,' called Ben, suddenly starting to run towards the gate.

'Come back,' shouted Bridget. 'Ben, come back at once.'

The car came in sight round the bend in the lane. It was a big, posh car, a new BMW. It roared into the yard and came to a screeching stop right in front of the farmhouse.

I saw Viv coming out of the house. She stopped at the top of the stone steps leading down. Bridget was already halfway into the yard. She'd grabbed Ben by the hand and he was pulling her along. I had almost caught up with them by the time the car door opened and a man got out. He was a young guy with slicked-back hair, a snazzy jacket and trendy trousers.

As Viv came down the steps, Bridget went and stood beside her, her red specs glinting in the bright morning sun. The man walked briskly towards her and Viv, then stretched his hand out, ready to shake their hands.

'Hello,' he said. 'I hope you don't mind. I'm a reporter from the *Western Post*.'

18

I remember total shock, like something horrible had fallen out of the sky. Bridget and Viv both looked stunned, though when Viv began speaking, she sounded quite calm. But I knew her well enough by now to suspect that's not how she felt. 'Uh-hu?' she said. 'And how can we help you?'

'Bob Martin,' the young guy said, leaning forward and holding out his hand again. 'News-feature reporter on the *Post*.'

Neither Bridget nor Viv responded to this or to his offer to shake hands. He just carried on talking. He said that in the last few days, his newspaper had been getting reports that there was a New Age community in the valley near Pen-y-Cwm. They'd already run a preliminary article. Now they'd like to do a full report. He hoped we would co-operate.

As he spoke, the guy was looking around. I could

see his eyes getting all satisfied as he took in what he could see of Greenland – us children standing there in the yard, the wood store beside the farmhouse, Viv and John's yurt in the meadow beyond, our yurt beyond that, the shower-tent, the roundhouse peeking out from the bushes on the left-hand side of the meadow. You could see the guy positively relishing the thought that he'd fetched up in the right place.

Now the man had said what he was doing in Greenland, Bridget replied with a laugh. 'Well, there are a few of us living here. It doesn't necessarily make us a New Age community. And anyway, what's it got to do with – what's your newspaper called? – the *Western Post*?'

'Well, put it like this,' Bob Martin continued. 'I'd say a lot depends on your reasons for being here. If you've got any thoughts you'd be prepared to share on that, talking to me would probably be worth your while. You know the way people gossip, the way false rumours get about. You wouldn't want the wrong kinds of stories appearing, would you?'

As Bob Martin was speaking, he turned back to his car and, leaning inside, brought out a copy of a newspaper. He handed it to Bridget and as she and Viv looked at the front page, he said Bridget should turn inside to page two. As she and Viv began to read, Viv leaning over Bridget's shoulder, the reason John came home so worried the other day filtered into my brain. He must have seen the paper in Carmarthen, when he was fetching our letters from our P.O. box.

Bob Martin didn't stay long. Bridget and Viv acted

as if the newspaper piece was really stupid. They looked at each other and giggled as they read some bits aloud, including stuff about London hippies living off the state and growing drugs, and local villagers who didn't want them around. But even though they made it clear that the newspaper had got it so wrong it wasn't worth contradicting, Bob Martin continued to ask them questions. He eventually left when he realised he wasn't going to get any answers.

After he'd gone, it was clear that Viv was upset. 'But what do they really want?' she kept asking. 'And how did they get to know about us?' Her tone of voice reminded me of that time she'd spoken to me about keeping the Greenland rules.

Supper that evening was odd, too. John had got back from Newcastle Emlyn where he'd gone to fetch some supplies. I was helping him carry in the sacks of beans and flour when Viv came over and took him off at once, calling Bridget to join her. Jeremy was not at home at that point, or no doubt they'd have called him too. Dad, of course, was away on his course and Greg and Nuala had only just left. Anyway, the three of them disappeared upstairs to the attic room we use as an office, where the old loft in the farmhouse used to be. They were up there for over an hour.

Supper was at the usual time. Viv had made spicy bean casserole. It had been cooking for ages, and we'd just started eating when we heard the sound of Jeremy's Landrover. Bridget got up from the table and went outside. I guessed she wanted to have a private word to fill him in on what had been going on. Jeremy had been away at a conference for several days and he and Bridget stayed talking outside for quite a while. By the time Jeremy came in the kitchen with Bridget and sat down to join us, he looked so serious.

Jeremy started what was to be a long discussion by looking round the table. His gaze seemed to linger on me, or was I imagining things? He said Bridget had told him about the newspaper man. He asked if any of us kids had been wondering about him.

'Not really,' said Matthew. Amy said, 'Yes.' I just shrugged my shoulders. Then Viv and Bridget both looked round at us and tried to sound reassuring as they each said they felt fairly sure that the man was just trying his luck and that he wouldn't be back. But then Jeremy tested us: any of us seen any strangers hanging about Greenland? I suppose I must have started blushing because I became aware of Matthew staring suspiciously at me. Luckily, Bridget started talking, and talking very loudly. She was obviously totally fed up. Her face had gone all red like her glasses and she shouted angrily: 'Newspaper reporters, what next? They have no right to come here asking questions. People must have the freedom to live the way they want to. That's what life is about. Ridiculous to come asking such stupid questions.'

Bridget's outburst felt so peculiar because she never usually gets cross at all. Every now and again, she teases Jeremy gently when he gets carried away and sometimes she gets quite intense. But this was different and when supper was finished, she and Jeremy vanished off to their roundhouse, telling Amy and Matthew they could play out for an hour, then it would be time for bed. They must have wanted to talk things through on their own. I found this puzzling then, and I still do now. I don't understand why grown-ups feel they've got to keep so much of their talk to themselves. Then again, I'm still not sure why I hadn't mentioned the pale-faced guy in the lane, the Man in the Trees as I'd begun to think of him. Or the man on the bicycle up on the road who'd asked me those questions some weeks before. I suppose partly it was because I hadn't said anything earlier, I didn't feel I could say anything now. Also, if I let on about the creep in the lane, I knew it would also come out about Megan, and I didn't feel like talking about her. For a start, I knew Amy would get all superior and assume that Megan was my girlfriend. I definitely didn't want that kind of response. Megan and me was something private, just for her and me.

So I stayed quiet . . . mum . . . silent . . . and I suppose that eventually it made things much worse. Because, of course, when the man from the *Western Post* came back, which he did, lots more events unfolded. My life in Greenland got really scary.

19

Saturday afternoon, I went up the hill to meet Megan as we'd arranged. When I got to the top, I lurked about until I saw her coming up through the field. We went in the cottage for a while and chatted. Then we went back down to the woods and played about among the trees. I told her about Bob Martin coming to visit. I said how strange it felt, having newspaper reporters coming to ask you questions as if you didn't have the right to be in the place you were living. She was sympathetic. 'It'll be all right,' she said. 'Don't worry. You've done nothing wrong, have you? It's bound to turn out right in the end.'

There didn't seem to be much else to say. Megan told me a bit about what she'd been doing at ballet. She also said she'd been rehearsing for the eisteddfod in the village and that she'd nearly finished learning her poem. In fact, she tried the poem out on me, in Welsh, standing on a tree stump like she was up on a stage. But she got mixed up when she came to the middle part of the poem and, when she went back over it and still couldn't get it right, she said she'd have to work on it some more.

That was it. My mind was somewhere else during our whole conversation and Megan obviously sensed this. I couldn't concentrate on what she was saying and suddenly it didn't seem like she and I had so much in common after all. So after a bit we said goodbye and agreed to meet up the following weekend. I said I'd come up to see her on the Saturday because the following day we were supposed to be going to Carmarthen to meet my Dad back from his course.

On the way back down the hill, I thought about friends. I was missing my old friends from school, that's for sure. Yet in a way, even though I'd just seen her, I was already missing Megan more: it was like we'd started getting to know each other, then today there was this horrible blank. I tried to reassure myself that there'd be other chances to meet and maybe by then the problems in Greenland would have sorted themselves out. Little did I know.

No sooner had I got back down the hillside and crossed the stream onto the rough bit of land before the farmhouse than I heard the sound of a car coming down the lane. It was him again.

When Bob Martin got out of the car, just like before he was carrying a folded-up newspaper. It turned out to be that day's copy of the *Western Post* and it looked like he'd folded it deliberately so no one could miss the headline: HIPPY COMMUNITY – LOCALS LASH OUT.

This time Jeremy was at home. Viv and Bridget had gone blackberry-picking and they'd taken Ben and Hannah with them.

Jeremy was working round the back of the old farmhouse when he saw Bob Martin arriving. He called out for John, who was in the carpentry shed, and they both took the reporter inside the farmhouse. When Matthew and I went inside to see what was happening a short time later, we saw that the door of the upstairs office was firmly closed. Matthew and I went out to play football but after a bit, we both slowed down.

'What d'you think's going on in there then?' Matthew asked me, hunching up his shoulder.

'Dunno,' I said. 'It doesn't look good, does it?'

After about an hour, Bob Martin came out of the house with John and Jeremy close behind him. He went straight over to his car and drove away.

Again that evening there was sober talk round the supper table. I remember we were using our oil-lamps for light. Sometimes we use the electric lights which are powered from our solar panels. But we all like it best when we use the oil-lamps, they make such wonderful shadows around the walls.

This was clearly a serious discussion. The grown-ups took turns making sure that we children all knew what had happened so far, though we'd probably all talked about it more than they thought. Even Amy had asked me what I thought was going to happen. That made a change. Normally she was so snooty, though since mentioning her to Megan, it had been in my mind that maybe she was just not happy. Something Matthew had said backed that up too. One afternoon when he was showing me his football stickers, he'd started talking to me about his dad. I already knew that his dad lives in Birmingham and sends him regular letters but Matthew suddenly started talking about going to stay with his dad. He said he goes a few times a year. 'Lucky for me,' he added, 'unlucky for Amy.' I asked him what he meant. He told me Amy's mum had gone off to India and hadn't been in touch with her for a couple of years. I suppose that would account for a lot. At least I know where my mum is, and that she cares about me.

One thing that came out over supper that night was what had happened to John shortly after Bob Martin had first come out to Greenland. Apparently John had stopped for diesel a few miles out of Carmarthen and the man who took the money at the till had started asking him a lot of strange questions. Where exactly did he live? Was it down Pen-y-Cwm way? Did he know the hippies down in the valley? Had he seen the hippy children that everybody said weren't going to school?

'I didn't give him much joy,' said John.

Viv giggled. 'Poor bloke!' she said. 'He couldn't have picked a worse person to ask his questions to, could he?'

Another thing we talked about was that article Bob Martin had brought with him. I asked Jeremy if we could have a look at it but he replied it wasn't really worth bothering about. Then he changed his mind. Getting up from the table, he ran up the creaky stairs to the office and seconds later, came back down with a newspaper which he slapped down so hard by his place that it made his beard flutter at the end of his chin.

'I don't think it will harm them to be aware of this rubbish,' he said, looking round the table at the adults. John said nothing, just looked worried. Viv was unusually quiet. Bridget nodded slowly, the light from the oil-lamp reflecting in her glasses.

'Maybe,' she said, and the others nodded too.

Jeremy reached behind him and picked up his reading glasses from the shelf next to the table. As he put them on, he said he would just read us some of the quotes.

'These are things that have been said by some of the people in this area,' he told us. 'Or at least,' he added, 'this is what the *Western Post* says they've said. For instance,' he began with a grimace, glancing at the front page, then turning inside, 'here is one of their little gems. "All of them are hippies. We don't want

them here, they're a bad influence on our children."
Then there's this: "You don't know what they're
getting up to, keeping themselves to themselves. If they
want to live here, why can't they be part of the area in
the normal way?" Normal is what he'd call snooping, I
expect.'

Bob Martin had tried using these quotes from local
people to get more information from Jeremy and John
about what we are doing at Greenland. Apparently he'd
asked how many of us are living here exactly, how
many children are included and if any of the children
have ever been to school.

'And I'm telling you all this,' Jeremy said finally,
looking over the top of his glasses at Matthew, Amy
and me, 'because there could well be more strangers
coming out here from now on, and all of us need to be
ready for it. Things will sort themselves out, but we
must be patient, and we mustn't get upset.'

The next day a TV crew turned up. They drove
down the lane and in through the gate. Then, cool as
custard, they got out of their van, held up a camera and
started filming. John was around and when he saw
them, he told them to clear off. This was private
property and they were trespassing.

The TV people came back again on the Monday,
though we only discovered this later when Greg and
Nuala arrived back from their trip. Before we'd hardly
had a chance to say hello to them, Nuala was
complaining, in her Irish accent, that as they'd come to
the turning into our lane, they'd seen a van parked on
the side of the road. 'The cheek of it,' she exclaimed.

'Imagine!' Just as they turned off the road, they'd noticed a guy with a camera and they were sure he was filming them as they went past.

The next day, Tuesday, a local authority officer arrived wanting to inspect all the buildings. He apparently said he had reason to believe that planning consent had not been received for some of the constructions on this piece of property, and he would be grateful to be shown round the land at once so he could make a preliminary assessment of the situation.

That did it! Viv, this time, got into a furious mood. Bridget looked really bothered and Jeremy appeared anxious and determined by turns. Even John was muttering, both to himself and to everyone else. We were all talking about what was going to happen – everyone, that is, except for Greg. He just laughed things off in that casual way he has. 'Ahh! Don't worry. It'll sort itself out.'

Nuala obviously did not agree. 'Yes, but Greg?' she said, sounding more Irish than ever. 'What if it doesn't? What will we do?'

But the thing that had been weighing on all our minds had already begun to happen. What my Dad called Bureaucracy had managed to get its nose into Greenland.

On Tuesday evening, Jeremy and Bridget started trying to persuade everyone to agree to a plan of action. They'd obviously been discussing it a lot together and both of them looked very intense. 'Ah-ha,' I thought, 'there's obviously nothing quite like a crisis to get everyone making plans.' But I still wasn't reckoning on the sense of panic that was rising steadily.

The local authority planning officer had arranged to return the next afternoon, Wednesday. Jeremy was convinced the other officials would follow. This was his main reason for suggesting we should take up Bob Martin's suggestion. 'Now is the time for us to talk to the *Western Post* and try to get as full a story as possible into the paper. That way we can at least try putting across what we're trying to do.' He said that if everyone was agreed, he'd get in touch with Bob Martin the following morning.

But the next day, it wasn't only the local authority planning officer that arrived in Greenland. A health and safety officer turned up as well, asking questions about the kinds of construction we were using, and what kind of water supply, and how about the disposal of sewage.

What with Bureaucracy and Bob Martin, life was getting kind of frantic. I couldn't help worrying about The Man in the Trees and if that had been the start of the trouble.

20

The next day Irina returned. She arrived in the morning in a dilapidated old car driven by a dark-haired young man.

'Zis is my G-O-O-D friend Zac,' Irina said. 'We timed things R-E-A-L-L-Y nicely. His wife had their new baby the day before yesterday. And now he's so kind, he's brought me all the way back here.'

It was great having Irina in Greenland again except

that by now events had gone so far it was impossible to tell her my private worries about them. Even when we were alone together, it just felt like there was too much to say. I didn't know where to start. The whole situation just went round in my head like clothes in a tumble dryer. Somehow, though, the cycle never stopped. My thoughts continued whirling around. If Dad had been there, things might have been better. But he wasn't, and I was upset by all the tension. At mealtimes, everyone was edgy. Even Irina felt it.

'When ZIS baby arrives,' she said that evening, looking closely at Nuala, 'everyone will feel R-E-A-LL-Y better. We will forget all zis R-R-I-D-I-C-U-L-O-U-S fuss.'

It was quite an ordinary thing for Irina to say, but it made me realise how much we were all being affected. It also struck me that after Nuala's baby was born, Irina would probably be leaving again, and this time would she be coming back?

So now I felt lonely as well as guilty and worried. I dreaded that all kinds of strangers – reporters or TV men or planning inspectors – could turn up at Greenland at any time they wanted. None of us would ever be able to relax any more, except maybe for Ben and Hannah. And even they were getting grizzly.

What would happen then to the way we lived? Maybe we'd have to pull down the yurts and the roundhouse and go and live somewhere else just as I was getting used to the place. Would we kids be made to start going to school and how would I cope with a load of strange children?

It didn't help that every day it was a bit too hot. I often escaped to the woods. Nobody missed me, apart maybe from Matthew, at a push. But even he had started spending a lot of time with his mother, the worry rubbing off on him, too. Each time I went into my den in the woods, I felt I had to face up to the same question: was it me that had started everything off? Either the old man on the bike or The Man in the Trees were at the root of those newspaper stories. Surely it wasn't Megan who had spilled the beans? Maybe she had talked to her parents or even to her sister Catrin. I couldn't feel definite about anything any more. Whichever way I turned it over, it seemed to me that I was at fault.

My den in the woods had felt like my bolthole before. But now whenever I sat inside, even when I squeezed inside the hollow part of the trunk, I realised how far it was from being a place to live in. It wouldn't keep rain out. There was no food store. There wasn't even a proper place to sleep. If ever I wanted to run away from Greenland, I wouldn't be able to survive there for more than a day.

Several times that week, I found myself wishing Dad was around. I thought once of asking Jeremy to get in touch with him at his course to see if he could come back early. But I realised that, in order to do that, I'd have to explain what was going on in my head. I couldn't face it.

Then one morning that week, I think it was Thursday but I can't remember exactly, yet another car came bumping down the lane. Irina and I were in the

99

middle of French. We'd spent about half and hour with Amy and Matthew practising general conversation. Now Irina and I were on our own. The visitor turned out to be an Education Officer. She said she'd come to find out how many children were living at Greenland, what kind of education we were receiving and whether the parents were registered for educating children out of school.

Viv had been working up on the roof when the Education Officer arrived. Now she brought her through the kitchen of the old farmhouse into the playroom where Irina and I were doing our French. She introduced her briefly. But Irina barely nodded before carrying on with our French conversation, her voice getting louder and louder as Viv showed the woman upstairs to the office. I think Irina wanted her to hear every single word of the French we were speaking. '*Eh bien, monsieur,*' Irina shouted, pretending I was a famous author and asking me how many books I had written. '*Combien de livres avez-vous écrit?*'

We carried on talking, Irina and me, me answering as if I was the author of dozens of stories, Irina asking me questions about my characters and plots and daily routines as a writer. But for once you could tell that even Irina's mind wasn't focused on what we were doing.

'E-R-R!' she suddenly growled. 'Inter-FER-ing! Spying! Why can't they leave things alone?'

I'd been talking about detectives in my role as a bestselling crime-writer. But Irina's thoughts were ground in reality this time: she meant the endless visitors who'd come bothering us that week.

'Now ZIS one,' she grumbled. 'She eez probably too DUMB even to listen to what we are saying.'

As things turned out later, we were all wrong about the Education Officer: in the report she wrote later she said she was impressed by the quality and quantity of the education we were receiving and as long as it was inspected regularly from then on, we should be allowed to continue with it. But that report was still a long way off on that day of her first visit.

I sighed, Irina sighed, then Irina suddenly burst out, 'S-T-O-P now! – we must stop N-O-W! – We'll continue our lessons in a little while when zis W-O-M-A-N has gone.'

I went to the woods and I went straight to my den. I sat inside the hollow tree and as the minutes went by, me fiddling about with the odd twig or leaf, I knew I seriously wanted to escape, at least till after my Dad had got back.

But where would I go? I thought again about staying in the den and not going back at all. The same worries went spinning round but I reasoned them out. Maybe it wouldn't be too hard to waterproof the den; it would certainly mean a good deal of scrabbling for suitable material. But at least I could try. If I started straight off, maybe the den would be ready by tomorrow. As for food, I could start stocking up right away. Then I could move in and not go back to the yurt for a couple of days. Give myself a breather.

It was then I heard Jeremy's voice in the woods. 'Charlie! Charlie!' First I heard his voice getting louder, then fainter. After a while, his voice came up closer again. 'Charlie, are you there? Are you all right? I just want to know you're OK, Charlie. Charlie, can you shout back to me if you're there? It's Jeremy, Charlie. Are you there?'

I wasn't going to reply. I didn't want to talk to Jeremy, I somehow felt too scared. I thought I would just sit it out. But then I heard Jeremy's boots crashing through the twigs in the undergrowth and his voice got really close. I wondered whether to come out of my den and maybe pretend I'd been sleeping. Suddenly it was too late.

'Hey, Charlie boy! This is where you are. Glad to see you. Been a bit worried about you.'

Jeremy came round the edge of the den. 'D'you mind?' he asked, hovering at the entrance, and when I said it was OK, he manoeuvred himself inside and crouched down on the ground beside me.

I suppose it was nice of him to ask if he could come in. But I felt awkward and strange when he was inside my den. Jeremy looked uncomfortable too. He looked physically out of place, with his long gangly legs, and he didn't seem to know what to say. He just said he and Bridget and the others were all aware that this week must have been tough on us kids. He was sure we'd be getting back to normal quite soon, so we mustn't worry. Whatever happened, it couldn't stop how we were living. And my dad would be back at the weekend, Sunday wasn't it? And it would all be fine.

The more he said, the worse I felt for starting everything off.

'OK, Charlie,' he said in the end. 'Just wanted to say those few things to you. That's why I wanted to find you. Good den you've got here, by the way. Don't worry, I won't tell Matthew or Amy about it.'

Then he began creeping out. On the way, he biffed his head on a branch and for a moment I felt quite sorry for him. He really didn't know how to handle situations like this, his head was usually so much in the clouds. So when he asked me if I was coming back now – 'or will you stay out here longer?' – I decided I'd better go with him; it might make him feel better.

We walked back through the woods together. As we were coming in sight of the stream, he put his arm round my shoulder just for a moment. His arm felt heavy, though I could tell he meant it to be reassuring.

'Funny old life, Charlie, don't you agree? The sorts of things that happen?'

'Yeah!' I nodded.

But I wasn't prepared for what happened later. I was walking over to Bridget's pottery, desperate to find something to do, when I heard two voices talking inside. One was Bridget, the other was Viv. It was me they were talking about.

'I just wish his dad was here,' Bridget was saying in a worried voice.

'Yes,' said Viv, 'it's very distressing. That Education Officer seemed quite a sensible woman. But what if she gets talking to some social workers? Will they want to come round too, to check on all the children? You know how careful they've got to be these days, checking in case children are being abused? And what if they do come round and Charlie's still in a state? You never know what they might think.'

'Yeah, you're right,' said Bridget, 'it doesn't bear thinking about. It would only take another stupid newspaper story about children being kept away from school in a secret valley to start everyone fantasising. Then who knows what might happen, especially since neither of Charlie's parents is here?'

I scarpered. I didn't want either of them to see me. As I made my way back to my yurt, I began worrying about all the terrible things that could happen. The social workers. Perhaps they would have to inspect me for bruises? The police. Perhaps they would have to arrest my dad for leaving me on my own. Or they'd take me away from Greenland and put me in a foster-home while there was an investigation?

By the time I went to bed that night, I no longer felt part of this place – not any more, not ever.

21

The next day finally did it for me. It was Friday and I'd started really looking forward to Dad getting back on Sunday. But in the afternoon there was another big fuss. A story in the local newspaper, not the *Western Post*, reported what one of the local Pen-y-Cwm people had said. His worries about our community had started when he'd come across a boy who lived there. That boy, he said, was obviously not happy.

It was Jeremy who came back with the paper. He'd gone specially to Carmarthen that morning to pick up a copy of the *Post* to check if Bob Martin had published the piece which we'd invited him to write. Bob had said Friday. But standing in the newspaper shop looking through the Friday paper, a headline caught Jeremy's eye: 'Tomorrow: The hippy community tells its own story.'

Right next to the pile of *Western Posts*, Jeremy saw the headline in the local rag. LOCAL RUMPUS OVER HIPPIES, it blared. Underneath was the story about the boy who didn't look happy.

Jeremy must have started looking for me almost as soon as he got back to Greenland. I was coming out from the entrance of our yurt and saw him standing talking to Matthew by the gate that led into our meadow. He was the other side of the gate, leaning against the gate-post, and Matthew and he were deep in conversation. Matthew seemed to be shaking his head. Across to the left, Ben and Hannah were playing together outside their yurt, rolling over and over on the grass with Mollie yapping around them, trying to get involved. I saw Jeremy looking in their direction, then I saw him turn towards where I was standing. He obviously spotted me at once. He came through the gate and started walking across the field towards me. As he came closer, his little beard flapping as he hurried, I guessed that something new had happened. I tried concentrating on looking casual.

'Charlie,' he said when he got close, 'd'you mind if I come in a moment? Just for a bit more chat?'

This was our second chat in two days and this time too, although I was not sitting in my private den in the woods, I minded just the same. Jeremy told me about the article. One of the people from Pen-y-Cwm had said that a few weeks back, he'd come across a boy from Greenland. 'Actually,' Jeremy explained, 'the paper did not say Greenland, they called it by its Welsh name, Glastir.' Then he went on, 'But that doesn't matter, it's what the man said that matters. He said he'd had a talk with this boy he'd met and the boy seemed very anxious and pale.'

'Now I realise that at the moment,' Jeremy went on, 'a lot of people are probably saying quite a few things that aren't actually true.' He said that was normal with human beings, and he wasn't worried about it. 'But,' he said – and it was obviously a big BUT coming – 'I *am* worried about the kinds of questions that officials might start asking about us. So I just want to get the position straight so that I can be sure of our ground.' Suddenly I felt like I was sinking into a hole and it made me so nervous – nervous that I hadn't said anything before, nervous of Jeremy's reaction, nervous of everything that was going to happen. There seemed to be no escape.

'Do you know anything about it?' Jeremy asked, straight out.

'About what?' I replied crossly. I didn't like the way he was going on about this. I just wanted him to stop.

'About what I've just told you, Charlie, of course,' Jeremy continued in that hugely patient way he has. 'Have you come across anyone from the village at all?

Maybe someone poking about up on the road, or even up in the woods?'

I shook my head.

'Someone who might just have seen you from some way off and made up the rest of the story?'

I pretended to be listening and it's true I was concentrating, though not on what Jeremy was actually saying. All the time he was talking, I didn't say a word and when he stopped, everything went quiet, the way that places do when something's not right.

After a moment, I just shook my head. I don't know what I was thinking, or even, really, why it mattered so much not to let on what I knew. But after a minute I went on to make things worse. I said, 'No, I don't remember anything like that.'

Jeremy tried again. He went back over the subject of the article, explaining the problems that might arise if some officials became worried about the children here and got it into their heads that they shouldn't be living like this. 'Are you sure you don't know where this report might have come from?'

'No,' I said crossly, 'I don't know anything about it.'

Jeremy eventually gave up and went away and that's when I started feeling really, really bad. If anyone had said to me, 'You're nuts!' I think I would have agreed. I think I *was* nuts, bananas, the whole fruit bowl. But I couldn't help it because at the time, I was starting to feel seriously frightened. A horrible daymare came flashing into my head like in a video scene. I don't know where the idea went when I wasn't actually thinking it, but whenever it came back I saw the same situation. A policeman had come down to fetch me. I'd have to go with him to the police station in Carmarthen, he said. They finally had to find out the truth and there was going to be an identity parade.

So there was me in the police station, lined up with about six other boys, all of us shooting glances at each other out of the corners of our eyes, trying not to look as if anything was wrong. Then in came that pale-face creep from the village, the one I'd seen lurking around in the lane. He glanced at the policeman and waited for the go-ahead, then with a smarmy know-all smile, he started walking along the line, staring at each of our faces. As he passed in front of me, he looked me straight in the eyes. His eyes gave out a cold, sharp glint. Then he walked on to the end of the line before pausing a moment and glancing across at the policeman. When the police-officer nodded, the guy came back and stopped opposite me. Lifting his finger, he pointed straight at me and said something in Welsh which I couldn't understand. Something like, '*Dyna fe!* That's him!' In any language, it was all my fault.

The image left me with such an awful feeling, I couldn't bear it. I couldn't cope with thinking how everyone in Greenland would know how I'd let them down, and how disappointed my dad would be. And it would only be a matter of time before the news would get to my mum. Every time I tried to push these thoughts away for a minute and read a paragraph more of my book, BANG, the identity parade was back in my head.

After a bit, I gave up trying to calm myself down and started pacing about in the yurt, back and forth, back and forth, and round the stove in the middle. I went outside. It was spotting with rain though it still felt hot and there was an earthy, leafy smell of Autumn. I walked over to the farmhouse and then went on to the vegetable garden. Viv was working there, weeding the permaculture beds. She looked up and smiled, trying to show she was calm. 'Hiya,' she called, 'how's things?' I realised I had nothing to say. I went back to the farmhouse. I noticed that by now Ben and Hannah had given up rolling around in the grass and were playing tag with Matthew in the yard. Mollie was still jumping up and down. I pretended I was busy and went inside. In a few minutes, I came out with a book as if I'd gone in there specially to fetch it.

A plan was beginning to form. I realised I couldn't stay in Greenland a minute longer. I certainly couldn't stand the thought of being there when Dad got back from his course on Sunday. I wondered about going up to the village phone-box and phoning Mum on her mobile. Maybe she could help me sort things out. Maybe she would come down to Wales and get me. I could wait in the village, or even walk to the next one. But even as the idea came into my head, I realised I couldn't do it. I couldn't worry Mum like that and I could never explain everything to her in a phone call, anyway. No, I'd have to get away from Greenland right now, while it was still daylight. I'd go straight up through the woods to Megan's cottage. When it was nearly dark, I'd go down to her house and try to let her know that I was going to run away. Then before it was completely dark, I'd get myself into the cottage and stay there overnight. The next day, I'd set off early and find my way to Carmarthen, walking, maybe, and then I'd get on a train. I'd travel to London, then I'd go to Mum's and explain it all when I got there. I'd need money for the train ticket and a torch for the night as well as some food to eat and a map of the Carmarthen area. I started to get ready at once.

22

I went straight back to the old farmhouse and into the pantry. I was still carrying the book I'd brought from the playroom only a few minutes before. In the pantry I put down the book and opened the tins where the cakes were stored. Fruit cake in one, carrot cake in another. Then I opened the drawer where we usually kept the paper bags. I remembered the time when I'd taken that piece of cake for tea at Megan's. This time I pulled out three bags from the drawer and put them on the shelf beside me. Then I cut big slices of both cakes and put them into two of the bags. Next I looked for the cheddar cheese which was usually left on the slate shelf in the pantry. I hacked off a chunk and put it in the third bag. I packed up my supplies in my pockets, hoping they didn't look obvious. Then I picked up another book from one of the shelves in the living room and went out down the steps. I tried to look as if I was in a hurry.

'Charlie, Charlie,' Ben and Hannah cried. 'Come and play football. Come and be our goalie.'

'Not now,' I said. 'Later, OK? I just want to finish this project I'm doing.'

'See you later then, Charlie,' Matthew called out. 'By the way, got some new stickers to show you. My Dad sent them to me.'

'OK,' I waved back as casually as I could. Then I was off to the yurt to fetch the other things I needed. I decided I was going to take my small daysack with me because the rucksack Mum had given me was too big. I transferred my food into it together with my torch, a map of Carmarthen and also a tube map of London which I remembered I had in my chest. I checked that I had Mum's mobile number, then put all my money in the front pocket of the daysack – I had £73 altogether. I stuffed in an extra sweater in case it got colder. Then I changed my trainers for my boots and put on my jacket in case it rained.

The day was already beginning to get darker by the time I got into the forest. It was spooky in all the shadows. I climbed up through the trees as fast as I could but several times I managed to miss my way.

When I got out of the trees at the top of the hill, I looked up the field towards the cottage. It looked very lonely up there on its own, no lights in the windows, no smoke from the chimney. I shivered at the thought of spending all night there.

First, though, I was going to have to try to speak to Megan. I decided to go far enough down the hillside to see if there were any lights in the farmhouse. I knew from Megan that sometimes after Mr Evans had finished the milking, he'd have to go to the village or the school or the nearby town to fetch Megan or Catrin from their rehearsals or clubs. Sometimes Mrs Evans would be out late too. Maybe this would be one of those nights.

Or maybe everyone would be at home and Megan would be up in her bedroom doing her homework. If so, maybe I could creep down to the farmhouse and throw something up at her window to get her attention.

The farmhouse was all lit up. I realised I didn't know what this meant – whether everyone was at home or only one or two people. I started down the track, keeping as much as I could to the side furthest away from the house and running for cover between the bushes and trees that grew alongside it as it came near.

As I got close, I was thinking how careful I'd have to be. If Blodwen came out, for starters, she'd probably start barking. Then everyone would know that something was wrong. And there was no guarantee that Megan would be on her own in her room. She might have a friend to stay, or her mother or father might be in there talking to her.

I got opposite the house, then quickly ran across the track and round through the vegetable garden to the back of the house so I could get under Megan's bedroom window. I listened hard. The window was slightly open and my heart sank as I heard talking from inside. There were two voices – Megan's and someone else. The two voices were quarrelling crossly. The one that wasn't Megan was asking where her new CD had gone.

I heard Megan shouting at Catrin that she didn't

have the CD, then the voice was muffled. A long gap was interrupted by Catrin saying, 'Hurry up!'and 'I told you not to borrow my things without asking!'

'Oh no,' I thought, 'this is going to take for ever.'

Then I realised that, any minute now, the dark was going to start getting to me. Either way, if I spoke to Megan or not, I was going to have to go up the hillside to the cottage in the pitch black darkness, then I was going to have to go inside there on my own.

I decided to make a run for it so I could get there before the dark had settled in. There was no point in waiting for Megan. In any case, what would I say? And what could she do about it? It would be better for me to be on my way to the cottage while there was still a chance I could see to get there.

I turned away from the farmhouse and started up the track. A few steps later, I slipped noisily on the gravel and a moment later I heard Blodwen starting to bark. I froze against the side of the path. But she only barked a couple of times. Then there was silence again apart from the occasional mooing from the cows in the shed on the other side of the house.

It was cold by now and I was ravenous. Nerves I suppose: it was only just supper-time. I decided I'd eat at least half of the cheese and one piece of cake as soon as I'd got inside the cottage and settled myself in Megan's tent. It would be a kind of reward.

The door of the cottage was hard to open as usual. I felt nervous as I shoved it: what if, for once, there was someone inside?

I switched on my torch. I shone it quickly from side

to side across the room – nothing unusual there – and then I started again, shining it slowly round every inch of the wall. I also went into the side room where I shone it round the funny stone stalls. Next briefly into the tiny kitchen. Nothing. Then I went over to the tent, picked up the corner of one of the curtains and pulled it back. No one inside there either.

I lowered my bag down onto the bed, sat on the edge and took off my boots. I left them on the floor just inside the curtain. Then, after propping up my torch so I could see what I was doing, I opened my bag and took out the packages. First I ate some of the cheese, but half of it didn't seem enough. I nibbled at the rest, all the time intending to stop so there'd be some left for the morning. But soon it was all gone.

Then I opened the bags of cake. I decided to eat the fruit cake tonight and keep the other for breakfast. I gobbled it down. Then there was nothing else for me to do except get myself under the bedspread and blanket and try to settle down to sleep.

The bed was as uncomfortable as I'd remembered and it was impossible to relax. I thought that playing some word-game in my head would help get me tired enough to sleep – some version of the story game. Making up a story would give me plenty of options.

The version I came up with was a set of objects – one to go with each letter of my name – then trying to connect them up in a story. I decided on chocolate for C, harpoon for H, aeroplane for A, raccoon for R, lantern for L, ink for I and envelope for E. At first I thought the story was going to solve itself quickly. It started really well.

There was a man who got stranded in the jungle after his single-seater aeroplane crashed. He was determined to find his way out of the jungle and get back to civilisation. All he had to eat was one bar of chocolate, which he had to ration. But as he was struggling through the undergrowth, something caught his foot and he fell heavily and broke his ankle. After that, he tried to carry on walking but he couldn't get far. He knew that soon he was going to die. He realised he must try to leave a message behind him for his girlfriend in case anyone ever found his body. He searched in his pockets and found an envelope in his inside jacket pocket. The trouble was he had nothing to write with. But as he got weaker and weaker, he decided to use his own blood for ink. He pricked his finger with a thorn, then started to write in drops of blood. His message was nearly finished when it started getting dark. Above his head, a raccoon was chattering. Then the raccoon ran away. He was losing consciousness when he heard the raccoon coming back. A moment later, he saw a glimmer of light. He thought he was hallucinating but the light came nearer till he saw a lantern and, shining in the light, a sharp harpoon. Finally he saw the face of a hunter. Was he going to kill him? Or was the hunter going to save him?

That's where I got stuck. I couldn't decide the answer. Then I started becoming aware of the silence all round me in the cottage.

23

I still couldn't get off to sleep. The mattress was hard and terribly lumpy and the bed-frame squeaked every time I turned over.

Then I began hearing a noise in the cottage. It came back each time I tried settling down in one place. It was just a soft noise in the darkness – like something slithering towards me, breathing deeper and deeper as it got nearer. Sometimes the breathing sounded incredibly loud and my heart would start pumping like I'd been running cross-country.

The same thing happened several times over and I was feeling really frightened when I realised it was just the sound of myself, echoing against the woollen blanket.

The blanket was old and itchy. When I pulled it up to my shoulders, I felt it scratching against my chin and that also stopped me from getting to sleep.

I was trying to get used to things when I heard another noise in the room. It was a kind of rustling. I sat bolt upright, fumbling around for my torch. At first I couldn't find it though it was supposed to be under the pillow. Now I had to feel around for ages before my fingers finally found where it was. With all my tossing and turning, it must have worked its way over the top end of the mattress because now it was squashed down between the mattress and the old iron bedhead. When I finally got it switched on, I leaned round the musty old curtain to shine it round the room. Nothing. That got me really upset. I had no idea now if I'd imagined the rustling or if there truly had been something out there in the darkness.

Suppose there was a living creature out there. It might climb on the bed, walk over the blanket, come up onto my face. But even then, I reasoned, it would be smaller than me. And even a rat would get scared, I supposed, if it suddenly met something much bigger than itself and alive, especially if that something sat up and shouted.

But the worst thing was not the idea that the creature would eat or poison or squeeze me to death – not like a lion or a python or a big brown bear. It was just the sensation of something skittery and wild, and knowing it could come so close in the dark that I'd feel it.

There was no chance now of getting to sleep. I resigned myself to a whole night of tossing about on the bumpy old bed that protested every time I turned over.

What I hadn't reckoned on was the wind. It started quite gently, as if it wanted only me to know it was there. Then it started getting stronger, stirring itself into a stormy temper, impatient at not being noticed. I remembered the drops of rain that morning and that it had felt a bit colder than in the previous weeks. Someone, maybe Viv, had looked up in the sky and said she thought the weather was going to change.

The sound of the wind became more alarming. Soon it felt as if the house would be blown down, the windows rattling. Then somewhere round the side, a door started banging. I was still trying to work out that it must be the door of the shed when I distinctly heard a tap on the window. It was a single short rap. My heart leapt into my mouth.

There it was again. This time I felt as if my whole body was bursting. Should I call out? Lie low? Get out of the cottage and run for the farmhouse or get under the bed and try to hide?

Tap . . . tap . . . before I knew what I was planning, I heard myself speaking. 'Who's there?' I called out. 'What do you want?' I couldn't help calling into the darkness, except that what came out of my mouth was scarcely a croak. I felt ashamed when I heard how pathetic it was until I realised no one else would have heard it anyway.

Then the sound came again . . . a single distinct rap like before; a pause, then once again. This time I held my breath until I thought I was going to explode. Then I suddenly remembered the funny little thorn bush I'd seen growing at the back of the cottage. I realised that if the wind was blowing against the house, it could easily be one of its branches forced by the wind against the window.

As soon as my brain had managed to work that one out, I began to feel really, really shaky. Knowing what the sound was made me feel worse. Now I found myself wondering what on earth I was doing in that old cottage. What if some dangerous criminal was to fetch up at the cottage – someone on the run or some weirdo just hanging about? I could be murdered up there and no one would know, not if the murderer strangled me or suffocated me so there would be no blood, then dragged my body out of the building and buried it down in the woods.

Besides, I started realising that, even if I survived

the night, there were going to be lots of other problems to face in the morning. I began going over what I was going to have to do. Get away from the cottage without anyone seeing me. Then get myself as far as Carmarthen and the station. Find the right train for London and Mum's. Again I wondered if I should phone Mum before setting out from Carmarthen. But what would I tell her? She'd probably try to stop me – and she'd be livid; with Dad for not being there and livid with me for telling lies.

No, I couldn't phone her. Instead, I began making a mental list of all the things that could go wrong. For a start, there could be a problem about buying a ticket. Are children allowed to buy their own train tickets? And if anyone was going to arouse suspicion, it was definitely going to be me since I look a bit young for my age. What if the man or woman in the ticket-office challenged me? 'What are you doin', laddie? Where do you think you are goin'? You'd better come round the back here and do some explainin'!' A man's voice booming out and me with no idea what I'd do in response, whether I'd try to run off or break down and confess where I came from. Yet I couldn't possibly confess that or Dad and Jeremy and the others would all get into trouble. Breaking the secret of Greenland was part of the reason I was running away.

Suddenly everything felt too much for me. I would love to have had someone to speak to, Mum or Megan or Irina or Dad. Now I wished I'd been bolder when I'd reached the farm that evening. Why hadn't I at least tried contacting Megan? I could have called out quietly under her window, or risked throwing up a piece of gravel. Then at least she'd have known I was there and she could have come up to the cottage in the morning to see that I was all right.

Somehow I had started to cry. I couldn't help it and I couldn't stop it. I just felt lonely and helpless and scared. As the wind continued to rattle the windows, moaning down the chimney and banging the door out the side, I felt like a person out at sea, alone on a ship that everyone else had abandoned. My face got wetter and soon my nose was disgustingly runny. I put my hand in my trouser pocket and felt around for the hankie I usually kept there. It had got all scrunched up under the bag of fruit cake and I think some crumbs must have fallen into it, because it smelt all sweet when I put it to my nose. Soon the hankie was wet through, too. Instead I tried wiping my nose on the blanket. But the blanket was old and had gone so hard, it didn't soak up the dampness. I had to keep on with my soaked-through hankie.

After a bit, I felt a bit better and terribly tired. I lay back down in the bed. 'Well,' I thought, 'I'm not dead yet. Whatever's going to happen will just have to happen. *Kay sera sera*, as Mum would say.'

I listened to the wind for what seemed like ages and gradually felt calmer. So it was then, I suppose, that I finally went off to sleep. Already I'd noticed the dark was losing its grip. Glimmerings of light were starting to peep through the window: in the morning, I thought, I was going to feel terribly tired. So maybe it was the idea of my own exhaustion that finally sent me to sleep.

24

I woke up knowing that someone was in the room. At the same moment, I knew for sure that I'd overslept. The air was stuffy and the room had that middle of the morning feeling, like when you've been planning to get up early and as soon as you wake, you know that you've blown it.

I knew someone was nearby, but I also knew it couldn't be Megan. It was someone heavy-footed, searching around for something they needed. I could hear clumpy boots and impatient clicks of the tongue. I lay unmoving in the bed, willing myself not to alter the position of a single muscle.

Eventually, I could hear the heavy footsteps coming towards the curtain. Almost at the same moment, there was a loud intake of breath. 'Duwcs!' a man's deep voice exclaimed. I somehow knew he was aware of me though at the time I couldn't work out how. Only later did I realise that one of my boots must have been sticking out from under the curtain. I knew for certain that I was about to be discovered.

The curtain was yanked to the side, and so hard that it got partly pulled off the string that was holding it up. As the material sagged onto the bed, I saw looking down at me a ruddy brown face which I immediately guessed must belong to Megan's dad.

His face looked shocked and angry and puzzled all at the same time. '*Beth yn y byd . . .?*' he started to say. His voice was Welsh and he looked like Megan. '*Beth yn y byd . . .?*' he said again. I was pushing myself back against the wall by now, propped up on my left elbow and he said in English, 'Now what's going on here, boy? Who on earth are you?'

I didn't know how to reply. I suddenly felt about as small as a two-year-old. All I could do was mutter something about being Megan's friend.

'A friend of Megan's, is it?' His voice had a dozen questions in it. I could sense he didn't really believe me and I dreaded that soon I was going to have to tell him where I came from and why I was running away.

'Come on then, lad, you can't stay here. *'Dere ma 'nawr, dere ma* . . . come on with you.'

Mr Evans reached forward a big strong hand. I didn't touch it, but I could see it looked as hard as iron.

'You'd better be getting yourself out of that lumpy old bed,' he went on. 'Then we'll be going down to the house to see if we can sort this out.'

25

On the way down the hill, I noticed that the track was wet. It must have rained in the night. The air was certainly colder.

Almost before we got into the farmhouse, Megan's father started calling: 'Ann! Ann! *Dere ma!*' He'd not said much on the way down the hill. Just once he turned to me, saying, 'This way, boy,' almost as if he was speaking to a dog. But I don't think he meant to be rude because he added, 'But you probably know the way already, hey?'

Funnily enough – and I liked him for this – he never tried to check on me to make sure I wasn't planning to run off, like by putting his hand on my shoulder or anything like that. I suppose he could see from my expression that I didn't have the heart to be going anywhere. All I could think of was that my plan had failed. To be honest I felt like a complete wimp.

Then when we got in through the side door and into the farmhouse, it was as if something changed – like I suddenly became an exhibit and he couldn't wait for someone else to see me.

'Ann! Ann!' he was calling and I heard the sound of Megan's mum calling back from upstairs. She sounded impatient, as if she didn't want to be bothered just then.

She came into the kitchen a minute or two later. Her eyes landed first on Megan's father, and then they landed on me, standing just behind him.

'*Pwy yw hwn?* Who's this?' she asked, her expression all bunched up as if Megan's dad had managed to catch something unpleasant and dragged it into her house.

'Well, I'm not sure of the answer to that, Ann fach. I don't know anything at all about the lad, except that I found him up in the old cottage and he says he's a friend of Megan's.'

'A friend of Megan's?' You could hear the disbelief in her voice. It was the astonishment of someone sure she knew everything about everyone.

'Well, he doesn't go to Megan's school. And he's not in the big school either, I'm certain of that. I can't think who he can be. I've never seen him before in my life. And anyway, what was he doing, hanging about in the cottage?'

Megan's father quickly turned the questioning on me.

He said sternly: 'Now boy, how about starting with your name and where you live?'

I felt very embarrassed. I half wished that Megan would come in the room. But I couldn't possibly bring myself to ask where she was. I couldn't even make myself speak.

'You better start answering now, my boy. Because before long, Megan'll be getting back home from ballet and her eisteddfod rehearsal and I'd rather know your story from you yourself before she arrives.'

I didn't know what to say. I was standing in front of the sofa at the edge of the rug in front of the fireplace. Megan's dad had moved back towards the passage that led out of the kitchen and was leaning against the doorframe. I looked down at the floor, my eyes fixed on Megan's dog, Blodwen, who was lying asleep on the same place on the rug as when I came to tea with Megan. My tongue felt heavy and my throat was dry. I just kept on thinking, 'This is it. Now I'll never be able to get away. I'll have to go back to Greenland and they'll find out what's happened and I'll really be in trouble.'

'Come on boy,' Megan's dad repeated. But I still didn't answer. In the silence a funny squeaky noise emerged from Blodwen. She was turning over and stretching in the way dogs sometimes do in their sleep, first making a little whimpering sound, then a low groany noise as they go back to sleep.

The interruption made everything else in the room

seem extra quiet. The grandfather clock was ticking away and I began to fear that this scene might continue for ever. But then the dog yawned and I couldn't help myself smiling. Unfortunately, that made me look up to see if anyone had actually seen me smiling, and that meant me looking over at Megan's mum who was still standing in the other doorway. So that's how I noticed that she was staring at me, her head tipped a bit on one side, looking exactly like mothers do when they're trying to put themselves in your shoes so they can understand how you're feeling but still keeping a bit of themselves separate from you.

She looked so like my mother at that moment that I couldn't stop myself from smiling some more. I knew I was doing it, because she sort of smiled back.

'You've probably forgotten it in all this fuss – your name, I mean,' she said.

'It's Charlie,' I burst out. 'Charlie Daniels. And if you want to know where I live, it's over at Greenland. Except that I'm not living there now, not any more.'

'Greenland? Greenland?' Megan's dad sounded astonished, as if he'd never heard the word before and couldn't get his tongue around it. 'You mean Glastir?' Then he glanced swiftly over at Megan's mum before looking back again at me. 'So where are you living now if you're not living down in Glastir any more? Sorry, I mean Greenland.'

'I'm not there because I've moved,' I quickly replied. 'And now I'm on my way back to London except that you're delaying me. Well, not you,' I said to Megan's mother. 'Mr Evans!'

Megan's father was now staring at me as if he was concentrating hard and all the answers would dawn on him shortly.

At that moment I realised that it's the same with grown-ups as with children: they want answers just like we do, and usually they want them at once, quick and simple and complete. So they can understand. And when they don't get them, it must leave them feeling impatient and disappointed.

'Yes, Greenland,' I repeated. 'I've been living down there. You know . . . the other side of the hill . . . down in the valley? The English people?' I added weakly.

I could see then that he could place me. New questions loomed up in his eyes now like moths flying round a light. The situation was not easy for him. How could it be, with a strange boy in his kitchen looking dishevelled and still a bit frightened? For exactly what was he saying? Was he running away? And, if so, what from? And how had he got to know Megan?

Mr Evans looked over at his wife.

'*Wrth gwrs*,' he sighed. 'Of course. But Megan?' His voice had an equal mixture of suspicion and interest. 'And you say you know Megan? She hasn't said anything about you to me.'

'I asked her not to,' I replied. 'Because it's supposed to be secret.'

'Secret?' said Megan's father. 'What exactly? It can't be much of a secret, can it, when everyone knows that you're there?'

Now it was my turn to look surprised. 'Not what we're doing in Greenland,' I burst out. 'No one knows

126

what we're doing in Greenland or the reasons why we're there, finding ways to save the future, nor that we children are there as well and we believe in it too.'

'Oh come on now, Charlie,' Megan's father said crossly. 'Don't be daft, boy. You can't tell me that everyone in this area doesn't know all about it. Well, maybe not every single detail, not your names, maybe, or all of your faces. Or exactly how many children you've got there. Or what you're doing exactly. But in general,' he emphasised, 'in general we *all* know.'

'That's only because of the newspapers,' I burst out loudly. I felt suddenly angry and very upset. 'They should have left us alone – them and the nosey parkers from the village, whoever they are. Maybe you know all about them too!' I threw at him accusingly.

'Now hang on a minute,' Megan's father came back at me, sounding a bit angry too.

Then Megan's mother interrupted.

'Look, why don't we all sit down and try and sort this out? It's a bit hard when we're all standing up like this, isn't it?'

That's when I clammed up again. Maybe it was because I could hear Megan's dad getting angry. Maybe it was because I began to realise I'd said too much already.

They both stared at me after we all sat down, me on the sofa, them in the chairs on each side of the fireplace. I could feel their eyes burning the top of my head and the back of my neck. I just looked at the rug on the floor, with the dog half in and half out of my range. I studied the pattern on the rug and spotted where there were dog hairs sticking up between the tufts. All the time it was like I was inside a bubble or even a spacecraft. There was air to breathe but I feared it would soon run out. And on the other side of the metal skin of the spacecraft, there was a vast and complicated universe that couldn't even start to comprehend what I was thinking. My mind raced across all the people who were going to be upset. My father, Jeremy, Bridget, Viv, John, Mum, Matthew, the local schools officer, even Megan – their faces would loom up in front of me and then I'd manage to push them away and they'd float away again.

The silence was extremely embarrassing. I could hear Megan's mother and Megan's father saying things to each other. Some of the things they said were in Welsh and directed at each other. Some of the things were to me, and in English. But whatever they were, I didn't let any of the words or sentences into my ears. I just listened to Megan's dog breathing. Also because I couldn't help it, I partly listened to the string of questions that came from the faces veering towards me from the other side of that bubble.

'Are you all right, Charlie?' – that was my mum. 'Why didn't you tell us?' – that was Jeremy. As for my father, he kept on calling, 'Charlie! Charlie!' like he was searching for me. The blessed twins just kept on asking, 'Charlie, will you come and play football?'

Megan's father and mother were still trying to get me to talk when Blodwen suddenly rolled onto her back, stretched all four legs in the air and, with a kind of yelp, rolled back; then she stood up on the rug and shook herself all over. I was waiting to see what she'd do next. Hey presto, she looked straight over at me, wagged her tail and started coming towards me. I thought it would have been obvious to anyone that she recognised me. But just then, Megan's mum got up and said, 'I'll let her out in the yard. Come on, old girl.' As soon as she heard her voice, Blodwen turned towards her and followed her down the passage.

At that moment, I realised I was bursting to go to the toilet. Could I ask if I could use their toilet? After my very long silence, that felt like an awkward thing to do. Besides, I was an intruder, wasn't I? How could I ask politely to go to the toilet when they probably saw me as some kind of robber or rascal?

But there comes a moment when you just can't wait.

'Sorry about this,' I said, my voice sounding incredibly loud, like a traveller who's just arrived back from a journey where there's been no one else to talk to. 'Could I possibly go to the toilet?'

Megan's father sat suddenly upright, like he was surprised I was able to speak. 'Course you can, boy, course you can. Sorry, I should have asked you . . . this way, this way, first door on the left.'

As I went into the little downstairs toilet, Megan's dad added, 'and maybe you'd like something to eat or drink as well. Course you would, I dare say you would. Must be hungry. Isn't that right?'

'Ann! Ann!' he shouted down the passage. *'Oes rhywbeth i fwyta i'r bachgen 'ma?'*

26

What happened next was really weird. Megan's father, her mother and me were sitting round the table with me eating a huge bowlful of Shreddies. There was a glass of orange-juice too, the freshly-squeezed sort that I like.

The two of them were watching me and asking questions in between mouthfuls. Questions like, 'And where were you heading to, Charlie?' 'And who were you going to find there?' 'And how were you going, were you going to walk?'

Listening to them was funny, because every time I started to answer, both of them would stop me, 'No, no, finish your cereal first.'

So I was still gulping down Shreddies, wondering if I'd be able to have a second bowlful when, out in the yard, there was the sound of girls talking and Megan came bursting into the room followed by an older girl who I guessed must be her sister.

'Uh! Uh?' Megan looked at me, she looked at her parents. Her eyes were bulging out of her head as if all of us were wearing green plastic noses.

'Charlie? Mam? Dad? What's going on? Charlie, why are you here?'

'All right, Megan, you'll get to know everything in a minute,' Megan's mother replied. 'And Catrin, everything's all right, you know. There's no need to look so surprised.'

Catrin was staring at me, then staring at Megan, then at each of her parents as if all four of us were nuts.

'*Steddwch lawr*, girls,' said Megan's dad, shifting up on the pine bench to make room for his daughters.

Catrin remained standing. 'Who's this then?' she said to Megan, gesturing towards me with her hand. 'Didn't know you had a boyfriend, Megan?'

Megan blushed and looked angrily at her. 'He's not my boyfriend, just a friend, that's all.' Then looking at me she added loyally, 'And a very good friend, too.'

'Now Megan and Charlie,' said Megan's father. 'I think you both better start explaining how you know each other, and how Charlie came to be sleeping in the cottage.'

'In the cottage?' Megan burst out. Then she looked as if she understood at least one bit of what might have happened.

'Charlie, is that where you were?' she asked me. I nodded. 'Last night?' I nodded again, shamefaced.

'Were you running away from Greenland, Charlie?'

This time I could hardly move my head, I just didn't feel like explaining. At the same time I knew it was all about to come out.

And it did, especially the bit about The Man on the Bicycle and The Man in the Trees and me getting so upset that somehow it was me that had put the local people onto the secret of Greenland.

Megan's dad showed a lot of interest. When I was describing the Man in the Trees that I'd seen in the lane up from Greenland, he began nodding as if he knew who I might be talking about. He shared a glance with Megan's mum and looked sympathetic. 'Harmless,' he said, 'that man is harmless, if he's the one I think you mean. But there you are, you weren't to know that. Just a bit of a loner, he is.'

Then when I got to the bit about the newspaper cutting that I'd seen in Megan's scrapbook, the one about the abandoned village that had been discovered in the woods, Megan's dad looked even more intrigued.

'Oh, you read about that too, did you?'

I said I had seen it, but I carefully didn't tell him where I had seen the cutting. I mean, I couldn't say I'd seen it in Megan's scrapbook because that would mean saying I'd already been in their house before and I didn't want to do that before checking with Megan.

Megan's father said he was interested in the abandoned village, too. He laughed. 'Maybe you'd like to go exploring there, would you? Sounds like the sort of thing you like doing.'

That's when I started to really like them both. I liked them even more when they'd heard most of my story. I say 'most' because, you know what it's like, there's always more that you think of later or even immediately after you've stopped. Somehow or other they must both have decided that what happened next had to be up to me. A lot of grown-ups wouldn't have thought of that. They wouldn't have sorted it the way Megan's parents did. OK, they made it clear that very soon they were going to have to get in touch with Jeremy or John or someone else at Greenland to let them know I was alright.

But they also said they'd like me to decide how this was going to happen. They couldn't just let me go off to London, it wouldn't be responsible. I was too young to go travelling about on my own with people not knowing what was going on. And they wouldn't just leave me to go back down to Greenland on my own. That would be too hard for anyone, they said, and they had to be sure that I got there safe. Also they'd prefer to help me by coming down there with me and helping to explain what had happened.

So they said I should have a think about it. Did I want them to go down to Greenland and fetch someone up to their house? Or did I want to go down there with one of them?

'Tell you what,' said Megan's mum. 'You and Megan can go up to Megan's room and talk it over while I get something quickly for tea. Then we can see what to do. And afterwards we'll get on with it without delay so everyone knows that you're safe.'

'Fried egg sandwiches all right for you both?' she called as we got up from the table.

'That'd be great,' Megan and I answered together.

'And Catrin, what about you? Or are you watching your waistline?'

Catrin all this time had been very quiet, first of all looking amazed, then pretty cheesed off, like someone who'd got left on the sidelines. Now she looked seriously disgusted.

'Oh Mam,' she said. '*Paid â bod mor ddwl!* Don't be so daft.'

27

It took only about quarter of an hour for Megan and me to talk things over before I decided what I wanted to do. Soon after, we'd eaten our fried egg sandwiches and I'd given my answer to Megan's parents.

Ever since then, I've felt really grateful to them both for giving me that bit of time to think things over because it meant that I didn't feel hurried or harassed or bullied. I just felt I could decide for myself.

It was coming up to five o'clock by the time Mr Evans and I got going. Blodwen was wagging her tail, walking back and forth in the way dogs do when they're waiting for their supper.

Outside the farmhouse, it was getting dark. There was that chill of real Autumn in the air, and the smell of dampness that makes you look forward to evenings round the fire. I realised I was wondering what my first winter in Greenland was going to be like.

As Mr Evans and I got into the Landrover, his wife leaned in through the door on my side and handed me a cake-tin. It rattled a bit as I took it.

'Welsh cakes,' she said, 'homemade of course. They're just a little something for your family and friends. Tell them not to worry sending back the tin. I'll come over and collect it in a few days' time.'

'Oh thanks,' I replied. 'They're nice, your Welsh cakes.'

But then I remembered that, as far as Mrs Evans was concerned, I'd never been anywhere near her Welsh cakes. So I didn't say any more and she didn't seem to notice. I just said thanks again. 'I mean, thanks for everything.'

Then Mr Evans put the Landrover into gear and we bumped off down the farm track towards the road. Megan and her mum were waving from the doorway. Catrin was nowhere to be seen, though the bass of some rap music was blaring out of her bedroom window.

All the way I was thinking about what Mrs Evans had just said. She was obviously planning to come and pay us a visit.

So things were going to be different. Whatever else happened when I got back to Greenland, the secret life of our community was well and truly broken. It wasn't going to stay hidden any more. The gap that I'd felt between it and the rest of the world was vanished. Gone. Finished.

Mr Evans switched on his full headlights. 'Nights have drawn in, that's for sure. Be Christmas soon,' he observed. I didn't reply. I was watching the track, thinking about what was facing me.

At the bottom of the farm track, we swerved onto the road. The road was downhill and the Landrover picked up speed. I was thinking we'd be at Greenland any minute, but oddly the journey took longer than I'd expected. First, after a bit, the road came to a bridge and I realised we must be crossing the little river that runs down through our land. Then we had to go up the other side of the valley to Pen-y-Cwm, then out of the village onto the road where there's the turn-off onto our lane. My heart was pounding as we drove down the lane. I don't think I've ever felt so nervous in my life, not even when I was trying to get to sleep in the old cottage and the thorn branch started tapping against the window. That was fear. This was worry about how they'd all react and what they'd say, worry about all the emotion.

Then I saw the police car. It was parked outside the farmhouse. No one was in sight.

'Well,' said Mr Evans. 'The boys in blue are here. Goodness me, they're all going to be glad to see you! Now Charlie boy, remember to keep your cool. Everything's going to be all right.'

Then, I'll never forget, Mr Evans turned towards me and winked. 'OK?'

At that moment, people came out of the farmhouse. First I saw Viv, then John, then someone that looked like a policeman though he didn't have his chequered cap on. They must have heard the sound of the Landrover and seen the lights.

Suddenly they were rushing towards me and I was out of the van and running over to them. Viv hugged me first. 'Oh Charlie, thank God, you're all right then.' Then John reached down and lifted me up just like I was one of the twins. After swinging me round, he hugged me again. I could hardly believe it, they seemed so glad to see me. I couldn't say anything, I just smiled like an idiot. Matthew and Amy were sort of hugging me too, and the twins both had their arms round my legs.

When there was a pause in all the hugging and shouting, I looked around for Mr Evans and saw that he was deep in talk with the policeman.

'Wel, wel,' I could hear the officer saying. '*Dyna ni, te, popeth yn iawn.*'

The policeman came up to John and the rest of us. 'Looks like the problem's solved for now, then. Very good thing too, very good. Of course, I'll be having to make a full report, have a good chat to Charlie to make sure everything's OK, follow up on one or two things, but I think there'll be time enough for that tomorrow.'

Then the policeman turned directly to me. 'Just want to ask Charlie here how he's feeling right now? Well Charlie, how about it? Feeling OK about staying here tonight?'

I just nodded and smiled. Inside I was thinking, 'It's not going to be entirely easy.' But what I said to the policemen was, 'It's OK.'

After the policeman had gone, we all went into the farmhouse. Irina was standing in the doorway and she hugged me a lot as we went in, but for once she didn't say a thing. I saw Bridget asking Matthew and Amy to take the twins to play in the roundhouse and suddenly they'd gone without any complaining. When all the rest of us got into the kitchen, Mr Evans looked around the room and smiled. 'Old place hasn't changed that much,' he said with a laugh. Then Mr Evans introduced himself to everyone and told his side of the story. You could see Bridget wanting to question him closely, especially when he got to the bit about giving me a bit of time to decide what I wanted to do.

'Couldn't you have got in touch sooner?' she asked Mr Evans at this point, leaning forward in that intense way she has. 'We've been so worried about him.'

'Not really,' Mr Evans replied. 'It took a while to find out the whole story, who he was and where he was from. So no, we couldn't have come over much earlier. After all, it was half past eleven, twelve o'clock, when I found him. Half past one, two o'clock, by the time he told us his name. Three o'clock, half past three, by the time we'd talked it all through. Four o'clock by the time he'd decided. Then, fair play, the lad had to have something to eat. So we got here pretty quick, considering.'

Viv and John were both nodding in rhythm. I could see them trying to understand and appreciate what Mr and Mrs Evans had done. But I could also see that they and everyone else must have had a very hard day and a hard night the night before. Irina was sitting next to me on the old sofa with me very close, and every now and then I could feel her squeezing my hand. Then Bridget started recounting to Mr Evans and me everything that had happened the day before when they'd realised I wasn't in Greenland and they couldn't find me, how they searched for me all evening even after it got dark, then again when it got light, and how they'd finally contacted the police that morning. The police had come quickly and checked the lane and along the road, and then they'd gone to the village to ask if I'd been seen. Then two policeman had come back down to Greenland to interview everyone there before putting a wider search into action.

As they talked, I felt really sorry for the trouble I'd caused them. Irina was sitting next to me, holding my hand, and after a bit I went up to Bridget and put my arms round her neck and hugged her.

'Sorry,' I said. Then I did the same to Viv and John, who were sitting close together, and when I sat down next to Irina again, she squeezed my hand especially hard. It was then that I really noticed for the first time that Jeremy wasn't there. When I asked where he was, John and Viv looked at each other as if they'd just remembered something important, and they told me he'd gone to fetch my dad.

'But I thought Dad wasn't coming back till tomorrow?' I said. They explained that when they were so worried about me disappearing, they'd gone up to the phone box in the village and telephoned Dad where he was staying on his course and they'd asked him to come back as quickly as he could. They'd done that in the morning before contacting the police.

'So your dad is on his way,' John added. 'In fact, he should be in Carmarthen by now. Probably he'll be here quite soon. And isn't he going to be glad to see you!'

'Hope so,' I answered, feeling a bit nervous myself.

With that, Mr Evans said he'd better be off. 'You'll have more talking to do when this boy's father gets back here, and you won't be wanting me in the way.'

I was really sorry to see him leaving. I felt by now – which has turned out to be true – that he was truly my friend, a kind of grown-up friend. I've seen him and Mrs Evans a lot of times since then. We've even been on a special journey together, me and him and Megan. But I won't say more about that just yet. I'll keep it a kind of secret till later.

Anyway, just after Mr Evans went out of the house, I suddenly remembered the cake-tin that Mrs Evans had given me with all the Welsh cakes in. I tried to remember where I'd left it. For a minute, I couldn't think. Then I suddenly remembered putting it on the bonnet of Mr Evans's Landrover after we arrived, just as everyone came running up to us.

I rushed out of the farmhouse as Mr Evans was getting into the truck. I tapped on the window beside him.

'What is it, Charlie boy?' he said, winding down the window. 'Decided not to stay, after all?'

'It's the Welsh cakes,' I replied, pointing at the front of the Landrover 'They're in that cake-tin on the bonnet.'

'Oh good, good,' Mr Evans called out as I picked up the tin and waved it at him. 'Hope you all enjoy them. And take care, Charlie. We'll be seeing you again in a day or two, no doubt.'

I took the cake-tin into the house. The roses on the lid looked perfect. A Martian looking at that picture would never have known that roses also have thorns.

As Megan's dad drove off up the lane, I felt sad and glad at the same time.

28

There was still a lot of explaining to do. Viv and John and Bridget kept going back over the events of the last couple of days. Viv and Bridget were doing most of the talking with John adding to something Viv had just said every now and again as he pushed his hair off his forehead. Irina kept patting my hand from time to time and smiling all over her face.

Irina didn't seem worried, only relieved. But with Viv and John and Bridget, it was like they couldn't quite get it settled in their minds. I reckon they were worried about whether they were responsible, and if not who was. I guess that I was worried about the same things too. You can never sort these things out exactly.

By now we were all waiting for the sound of Jeremy's jeep. Viv and Bridget would quieten between their bursts of questions. They'd both look down at the floor, then think of something else. John kept nodding, then shaking his head, then pushing his hair off his forehead again. I was feeling scared of Jeremy finding out the whole story and also wondering how my dad was going to take it and whether he was going to be angry or disappointed or just glad that I was safe.

When the expected sound arrived, part of me wanted to go rushing out at once. Part of me held back. But before I knew it, Bridget was already out there and I could hear her saying, 'It's all right, he's back, everything's OK, he's OK.'

Then suddenly Dad was rushing in. And at the very same moment – it was the greatest surprise – Mum was coming in as well. At first I just couldn't believe my eyes. 'Charlie,' they were both saying. 'Charlie, you're OK.' Mum was hugging me. Dad was hugging me. And I was hugging them both. Then Dad was wiping tears from his eyes. Then Mum was crying and laughing all at once and getting out her hankie and passing it to me because I was crying too.

Then the three of us sat down close together on the lumpy old sofa and Irina and Viv and John and Bridget took Jeremy away. They said they'd tell him all that had happened. And they left us to it.

From then on everything was fine. It really was. It turned out that Dad had rung Mum as soon as Jeremy got in touch that morning to tell him I'd disappeared. Mum had insisted on coming to Wales with him at once and they'd met at Paddington station with just a minute to spare before the train pulled out. Mum said it was the longest journey she'd ever made in her life.

Somehow, with Mum and Dad there, everything slotted into place. No one was cross, not Mum or Dad or me, even though Mum got impatient when it got to all the secrecy stuff. She just couldn't understand why Dad and the rest of them hadn't made friends with everyone in the area and why it had been so important to keep things hidden. When she did eventually start to understand some of the reasons, she could understand why I'd had the heebie-jeebies about thinking I was responsible for letting out the secret. When Mum understood why I'd felt so bad, and why I couldn't talk about it, Dad started getting the hang of that too, so it ended up with him really sympathising with why I'd started feeling so weird.

'It was bad timing too,' Dad added '– me going away on that course just when you were so new here, Charlie. I'm really sorry I did that. I was taking too much for granted and I didn't realise how hard it might be for you getting used to this place.'

'Well, it's natural Charlie would have found it hard,' Mum added. 'He's a thinker, aren't you, Charlie?'

I couldn't believe how good it felt to have the two of

them listening and really, really understanding. It made me think of Megan's father and mother too, and for the first time in my life, it felt to me that grown-ups can do it if they really, really try.

After a bit, Mum said I looked tired and was I ready to go to sleep. When I said yes, she asked Dad if she could sleep somewhere near me. There was a spare place in our yurt anyway, so she could have a mattress right next to mine.

Mum sat on the rug next to me when I got into bed, stroking my arm under my blanket.

'I'm sorry, Charlie,' she said at one stage, just as I was drifting off to sleep. 'I'm so sorry for all your trouble.'

'What trouble, Mum?' I asked her, because by then it didn't seem as if there was any trouble at all. Nothing felt out of place. Life felt as kind as the little breeze that was gently swaying the canvas sides of the yurt.

'Oh, everything, Charlie,' Mum replied. 'I'm sorry about everything that's gone wrong in your life – about me and your Dad not being able to carry on being married, about you getting unhappy after you came here to live, about you running away . . . you know, the whole caboodle.'

'It's all right, Mum,' I said. 'It's all right now. Everything is all right.'

As I drifted off to sleep, I could hear her breathing and, just for a moment, I remembered how frightened I'd been up in the old cottage when I heard my own breath echoing under the blanket and I thought there was some creature nearby.

Then I felt this great sense of relief about how well it had all turned out. I think I was smiling when I went to sleep.

29

The next day breakfast was crazy with everyone talking at the same time round the breakfast table. Ben and Hannah were asking lots of questions like, 'Charlie, where were you?' and 'Are you going again?' Amy surprised me by being really nice: she looked like she understood. Matthew was quiet but I could see he was relieved I was back and he and Amy both seemed interested to see and talk to my mum. I was telling Mum their names when I realised that Greg and Nuala were not around. I hadn't seen either of them the night before and they weren't at breakfast either. I was just on the point of asking where they were when Greg strode into the kitchen. He put out his hand, took mine and shook it before I even realised what he was doing. But this time, he didn't tease me. 'Good to see you, Charlie,' he said. 'Good on you, boy! They came over last night to tell us you were back. Nuala sends her best. She's having a lie-in this morning.'

Afer breakfast, Mum insisted that she and Dad and me should go up to see Mr and Mrs Evans and Megan. 'We must thank them for looking after you, Charlie,' she said. 'I expect you'll be wanting to tell Megan how things have worked out and anyway, we must thank Mrs Evans for the tin of Welsh cakes. And we'd better get going before that policeman arrives to start his report.'

When Dad and I reminded Mum that the policeman had said he was going to come in the morning, she said OK, we'd have to wait and when the policeman arrived soon after, there was obviously lots more talking. But by lunchtime, the policeman had finished and we were discussing whether we would go up to Mr and Mrs Evans's farm by driving there along the road or whether we'd walk up the hillside. After Dad and Mum said they'd like to go there my way, we realised there was a bit of a problem. Mum laughed about it. 'I've got nothing to wear,' she giggled. 'It didn't occur to me, coming away in such a rush, that I'd be needing country clothes,' she said. 'Not in the circumstances!'

So we went over to the farmhouse to find Irina and Irina said she'd come across to our yurt and lend Mum a jacket and some boots if they fitted. Mum was trying the boots on – 'And they do fit,' she was saying – when we heard Greg's voice out the front of the yurt. He sounded very impatient.

'Irina? Irina? Are you there?' Greg was shouting. When Irina went out, we heard Greg saying that Nuala needed to see her at once.

So that's how things were when we went up the hillside, Mum wearing Irina's dark red boots and her multi-coloured jacket. As we went, there were plenty of things to explain to Mum such as how I'd got the stepping stones into position across the stream and how I'd decided where to make my den and how I'd managed to make a way up the hillside. We had so much to concentrate on that we didn't think any more about what might be going on down in Greenland.

Megan was quite shy when she saw us but Mr and Mrs Evans were really welcoming, even though Mr Evans had obviously been lying on the sofa having a Sunday afternoon sleep. The TV was on – a sports programme. But Mrs Evans insisted we should come in and sit down and have a cup of tea. Then she said we must see round the farmhouse. By then, my mum and dad had introduced themselves to her and Dad had explained that they were divorced and told her all about my mum coming down from London with him because she was worried about me. But Mr and Mrs Evans didn't seem a bit bothered about them being divorced and soon everyone was chatting and, before long, Mr Evans turned the sound up on the TV and he and Dad were watching the rugby.

That's when Megan and I went out to look at her gerbils. It gave us a chance for a bit of a chat. We didn't say much about what had happened but I did ask Megan if she'd teach me to say Nos and Dydd with the proper pronunciation. That got us talking about me learning Welsh and I said I'd be keen to have a go.

'And you know what?' I said a little bit later. 'One day maybe I could come to visit your school when you're having an eisteddfod or a concert or something?'

After we'd all had tea and looked round the farm, Mr Evans said he'd run us back down to Greenland. By now it was getting a bit dark. So we all got in the Landrover and Megan came with us for the ride.

146

A big surprise was waiting for us when we got there. As we got out of the Landrover, we saw Viv rushing across the meadow, Mollie at her heels, heading off in the direction of Greg and Nuala's old bus.

'It's so exciting,' she called back when she saw us. Then waving her arms, she beckoned us over. 'You'll never guess what's happened!' she said as we stood there by the gate. For a minute, I couldn't think what she could mean. But then we heard the sound of a baby crying.

'It's the baby!' I called. 'The baby's arrived.'

'Yes,' said Viv, 'and you can come over to see her later on.'

So that's how we increased our numbers in Greenland and made friends with our neighbours all on the same day.

After that, things changed quite quickly. After being a bit suspicious at first when he came down to visit our land, Mr Evans soon started getting interested in all the renewable energy planning that was being put into practice at Greenland. He liked the permaculture beds. He liked the compost toilets. He loved the way the roundhouse was built and that made Jeremy especially happy. He was also very interested in the coppicing techniques that Jeremy and Dad had been using in our woods and, after a couple of visits, he started talking about the local technique of weaving hedges. 'I'll show you how we do it if you want,' he told them.

Then things got even better over the next couple of months when some of the other neighbouring farmers also started showing an interest. For instance, just a week or two ago now, Dad organised a day down in Greenland for local people to try out some of his ways of managing wood and for us to learn more about their skills. It was a great success. About six or eight farmers turned up and Ben and Hannah were in their element. There were people to talk to all day long.

Another thing that was especially important to me was that Mum started coming down to Greenland more often. I knew she and Dad would never get back together again: they both had their own lives by now. But it felt good to me that they could be so friendly. One day Mum even said, 'I think I'm starting to like the cold.'

And learning Welsh changed things too. The sessions were up in Newcastle Emlyn: people who speak Welsh and those learning all meeting together. There were some nice kids there, so I started getting new friends and soon I wondered if it might be time for me to start going to a local school. I mentioned it to Dad and now it's all fixed up. Soon I'll be starting at the local secondary school.

The last big thing I want to report is in one way the most exciting. Mr Evans and I looked into the story of that village abandoned in the woods. I started thinking about who might have lived in the place and making up stories about them and Mr Evans dug around in the library in Carmarthen, rooting out old books and papers. I think he was hoping there might be a family connection between him and the people who had lived in that village because, quite a long time ago, he says, there were some Quaker people in his family tree. He doesn't know for certain yet and, as he often says, he may never find out. It's interesting just the same.

We made an expedition to see the ruined village. Mr Evans took Megan, Catrin and me. After writing around a bit to try and find out exactly where it was, he'd managed to get in touch with the photographer who had taken the picture in the paper. When it turned out that Mr Evans knew someone who was related to the photographer, that proved a big help. The photographer sent Mr Evans his map, marked up so we could track down the place for ourselves. We actually went there last weekend. Catrin pretended to be bored most of the time, but we had a brilliant day. Mr Evans parked the Landrover where the photographer had suggested and we set off into the woods. They were dense in places and you could tell from the atmosphere that we were excited about what we might discover. I made us all laugh. I wasn't really thinking about anything in particular; I just suddenly said, as we were walking along, 'Woods are good. You don't know where they lead.' When I heard the others laughing, I thought about everything that had happened. Then I started laughing too.